CHANGELINGS

MELISSA MURRAY received the *Eric Gregory Poetry Award* at the age of 22. Over the last ten years she has written extensively for theatre and radio. Her plays have been produced in Bristol, Edinburgh, Australia, but mostly in London. She has received two writers bursaries from the English Arts Council and in 1985 won the *Verity Bargate* award for her play *Coming Apart*, subsequently published by Methuen under their new *Theatre Script Series*. In both 1986 and 1987 she was shortlisted for the prestigious *Susan Smith Blackburn Award* (Theatre). This is her first collection of short stories.

First published in 1987 by
Attic Press
44 East Essex Street,
Dublin 2.

Murray, Melissa
    Changelings : a collection of short
    stories.
    I. Title
    823' .914 (F)   PR6063.U742/

    ISBN 0-946211-42-6

Cover Design: Keggie Carew
Typesetting: Grafton Graphics
Printing: O'Brien Printing, Dublin

CHANGELINGS

Attic Press, Dublin.

TO URSULA

Contents

Space Invaders

Colette had just got the stock right when the news came over the radio that the aliens had landed. They had landed just north of the Naas dual-carriageway. For a second she stood, her wooden spoon dripping round brown stains on the cooker. Automatically she reached for the dishcloth to wipe — 'Pardon?' she said to the radio. 'What did you say?'

Obliging, the radio repeated its message, adding that there was no cause, whatsoever, for alarm. Emergency procedures had been established and were being implemented. Responsible citizens were urged not to panic, to remain where they were. The radio went on: 'The roads must remain cleared for use by the defence and security forces. We urge all citizens to drastically restrict their use of electricity and above all not to use the telephone. As will be appreciated it is essential —'

There was the sound of a thousand insects eating their way through cotton-wool, then silence. No amount of turning any knobs increased or decreased that silence.

She sat down at the kitchen table. Facing her were all

the ingredients for a good rich stew. There were rounds of onions, precisely segmented slices of carrot and turnip, thick lumps of potatoes. On the wooden board unfloured meat, too brown to bleed, was piled high. She looked at herself in the glaze of the casserole dish, an earless goblin gazed back. It was all ridiculous.

'It can't be true,' she said. It was irritating how weakly she said that. She looked at her watch, it was 3.17 pm. 'Perhaps there's something on the television?' Her voice had the habit of going up at the end of a sentence, but if she was asking a question there was no one to answer. That thought occurred to her.

As she stood up all her blood seemed to fall down to her feet. There was a sudden spurt of sweat on her upper lip, thank God she had a blouse on under her jumper. She ignored the weakness and dizziness of her body and walked, almost steadily, to the lounge.

Everytime she walked into the room she regretted the cane suite. It had looked so smart in the showroom but somehow in a house it was light-weight and insubstantial. Sitting on it, every move made was commented on with a crack or extended creak. Billy had never liked it, it had been her choice and now she could never complain. She knelt on the carpet fumbling for the plug while the wide glass eye of the television looked over her shoulder and into the middle distance. It took her a while to get the three prongs of the plug inserted, but finally they fitted into the socket. She sat back on her heels and was rewarded by the crisp outline of a newsreader miming at her. He was the handsome one with the head shaped like a peanut. The set always took too long to warm up.

'. . . as yet unexplained. It is certain however that the entire area has been cordoned off. In response to enquiries by the Government both the US and Soviet —' Abruptly a test card flashed up, then flickered out again. The newscaster looked distressed. 'I'm afraid we appear to be having . . .' Blank screen, silence, just the sound of residual electricity fizzing in the set.

She snatched the plug out of the wall.

'I wish I smoked,' she said. He hands looked helpless in the lap of her new jersey skirt. She wanted to be able to get up and over to the sideboard, pour out a stiff whiskey and slug it down with her head tilted back. Worrying about the heartburn it would give her seemed so trivial. She sighed and went over to the mantelpiece to wind up her grandmother's clock. She kept winding it, turning the key round and round.

This is serious she said to herself. She could be certain that her body was reacting but her mind, she knew from experience, could not be relied on. It had the habit of skittering off in the wrong direction, she thought sternly, this isn't a joke. But wasn't there something about an actor once, in America, reading something over the radio about Martians landing and everybody going crazy and panicking — what was his name, now? Not Oscar. There was something burning in the kitchen.

It was the stock. It had bubbled over and burnt itself all over the red ring of the element. She heard herself making cooing, comforting noises as she wiped the cooker clean and let the cold water trickle slowly into the scalded pan. It was Orson Welles, she thought with satisfaction as she put the kettle on.

'Electricity,' she said guiltily, and went round the room severing every appliance from its supply, even the fridge-freezer. It'll flood all over the carpet, she thought, but somehow she couldn't care. The room was absolutely quiet except for the hoarse, foggy whistle of the kettle. This must be her last cup of coffee, she decided as she put two spoonfuls of powder into her mug.

She cleared a corner for herself at the far side of the table and sat down. First she wrote on the pad with a topless black biro the number '1'. For the children. They're both at school, thank God. The Civil Defence or whoever it is must have the evacuation of the schools as priority. For the time at least they were better off there than with her. She had a desperate image of running down a long lime-treed avenue with suitcases and two terrified children while at their back the city flared into ruin. Next, she thought firmly, she must be practical, she must not panic uselessly. Billy — he would have reached some safe haven, he must have heard the news, he always travelled with the car radio up and blaring, he's fine. And the relatives . . . there were too many relatives, his and hers all over the place, she couldn't be expected to worry about all of them, that was what the Government was for. By the side of the third numeral she drew a question mark to signify herself. What was she to do? While she was thinking of that, the pen began drawing a series of gold-fish, one after another. How had it happened that here, in this country, in the middle of her life, something so extra-ordinary had happened. She tried to picture the incalcul-able distance of interstellar, intergalactic space. Where had they come from and why with so many worlds to choose, and in this world so many places to pick, had they landed in a farmer's field in Naas, Kildare? She laughed and that laugh made her get abruptly to her feet. In old Sister Agnes's voice she said, 'Do you not realise that this is real history, not dates and dead lists of foreign kings but the life blood of your own people.' But Sister Agnes had been talking about something else, she thought, and was surprised by the impulse to hide underneath the table. Or to run coatless out the door.

'I had better start packing.'

It was time for action. The most likely evacuation centre was Galway. There were vast granite caves there with their own water supply. Probably there were already caches of food in place, rice and so on. Dried apricots to prevent scurvy; she had always insisted on Aisling and Eoin having plenty of vitamin C. It would be a comfort to have the Atlantic at their backs. The bedroom was cold and the windows watery with condensation; the playing fields outside looked like those paintings people bought prints of. She opened her own chest of drawers and began pulling out the underwear. She took a pair of pants for each day of the week and one extra, three bras, a couple of vests and the unopened three-tights pack she had bought last week. Everything fitted on the dressing-room stool. It was covered in brown imitation silk and a scattered layer of talcum powder. For about a minute she thought of the various pieces of luggage in the house. She decided to pack the lot in Billy's extra-large holdall. It would be more convenient than a suitcase, she reasoned.

It was when she was standing looking at the folded rows of clothes in the hot-press that she began to feel real fear. The strong smell of clean clothes triggered it and she longed for her mother. She wanted uncomplicated, comforting, unquestioning love. She wanted to be six years old in a bright sunlight kitchen with her mother handing down soft boiled eggs and buttered bread for dipping. Her eyes filled with tears. What am I, nearly forty, she wondered, why am I a wife and mother? She thought of herself, her thin hair the colour of smoked haddock, her thin body with feet and hands as full of bones as those inedible, expensive fish. And the mouth, she thought savagely, don't forget that thin string of a mouth, twang, twang out of time. Oh why was he never here when she needed him. He was never there when being a man might be useful and appropriate. He was in a bar saying, 'Now, did you hear this one, this is great, this one. Well it seems there were two aliens. . .' She prayed, fervently to God he was in a bar somewhere. It was one thing to feel angry with a person, it was another to wish them dead.

'Pull yourself together,' she advised. There was saliva on her chin. She carried everything that was hers from the hot-press back to the bedroom, her knees making small snapping noises as she walked. 'There is nothing to be afraid of.' The pile of clothes slumped across the counterpane.

She thought about the aliens. In the movies aliens slid down the gangplank shapeless and glistening like old men's gob, or they'd appear segment by quivering segment. She didn't care. She didn't care what they looked like. She thought of tight-waisted abdomens sagging between rows of hairy legs, clicking jaws and eyes stretched up on stalks. Not spiders, she prayed to the merciful God, not that, and felt the unexpected loosening of her bowels. But why would they be ugly, she asked herself, and began to unhook her dresses from the wardrobe. Perhaps they would be beautiful, so beautiful they wouldn't wear clothes at all. There was a mound of crocheted cardigans; her mother persisted in giving her a new one every Christmas, in ever more delicate pastel shades. The clothes depressed her. She thought someone called Colette should be small, brown and vivacious. She should wear bright orange, clashing jewellery, and love the sun. She would enjoy the odd drink, and smoke excessively. She would be devoted to her children.

'I am devoted to my children,' she said defensively.

She sat on the edge of the bed, resting her shoulders, the back of her neck, her head against the pillow. Inside her mind, separate thoughts skimmed and circled round each other but refused to coalesce in a chain of command. Although not tired, she began to fall asleep and was half-dreaming of her old camogie team. She seemed to be running, flashing up and down the field, hearing her voice echo in the open air, while all the spectators were speechless. She woke up caressing the crack on her shin bone.

She must be practical, she thought, as she stepped out of the circle of her skirt, leaving her shoes in the centre. As she pulled the jumper over her head she smelt the thin winey smell of sweat.

'I must have a bath.'

Out in the corridor, her blouse unbuttoned, she forgot for the merest second where exactly the bathroom was, as though it wasn't opposite Eoin's room, as though it wasn't always opposite Eoin's room. There were only four rooms upstairs anyway, five if you counted the hot press, but that was too small to really be a room. She turned on the hot tap and the geyser ripped and roared into life.

Resting her head on the rim of the bath, her whole frame was free to float all the way down to the tap end. Pleasure spun all the way to the fringe of her fingers and her gently waving toes. In this programme on evolution she had seen once, it explained how all life had begun in warm soupy oceans and she could see the sense of that, though not why anyone had bothered to leave. Sighing she began soaping down the length of her body. 'God you're tall,' people would say peering up, squinting and shaking their heads. It wasn't easy to know why, to know if it was in admiration or disapproval. 'Yes,' she'd say. 'Must be six foot. Are you sure six foot?' they'd persist. 'Not quite,' she'd say, trying not to blush. Not that she did blush, rather she blotched, her skin discoloured with a rash like distemper. 'Not exactly six foot.' But they always looked doubtful.

She was drying herself in a leisurely way, patting the back of her knees, humming a little, when she was struck with a feeling quite like claustrophobia. Hardly waiting to wrap the towel round her she ran out of the bathroom, down the stairs and into the silent kitchen. The defrosting fridge-freezer dripped noiselessly onto the carpet, the clock on the cooker no longer kept time and the radio, full volume, blared out in silence. There was no news. There would be no news. She walked round the room skimming her fingers along the work surfaces.

Outside the sudden spring of a thrush's song came on and on like the trapped tune of a music box. The skin on her bare shoulders shivered. On the table in the corner, away from the food, was a piece of paper. On it was written her children's names, her husband's, a question mark and a line of fish facing to the left. It offered no clue to anything.

What were they doing here, what would they do with this? She looked at all the inanimate objects pityingly. Nothing could be more innocent than that toaster, less assertive. It doesn't deserve to be treated so off handedly. She was certain that the aliens would look with contempt, amazement, at this grubby wholesale little planet. They would offer, gently, their incredible, their marvellous machines. Shaking their heads, or whatever it was they had, they would redistribute wealth, abolish sickness, grant immortality, spiritual enlightenment and peace in our time. There was something about the idea that made her feel very peculiar.

'I'm cold,' she said. 'I can't stand here all bloody day with just a bloody towel on.'

Up she marched and back to her bedroom. Tweed skirts, cardigans, jersey dresses in a mixture of shades were piled on the bed in a graceless bundle. What she wanted, what she needed, was an outfit in hard, dark, black, black trousers, jumper and black knee-length boots. She should have the red rope of a bandanna round her head. This was an occasion she should dress for, but there seemed to be only a green pair of corduroys and a sweater machine-knitted by her cousin that she had been over-charged for.

The telephone rang. It rang loudly. It rang in every nerve and bone in her body, it rang on and on like a sullen child, like a sullen insistent child. The phone was on Billy's side of the bed, it would be Billy phoning to re-assure her, to ask for reassurance. It could be the army to tell her he had been killed or kidnapped. She could have no assurance as to whose voice she would hear if she lifted the receiver.

'Don't be a fool.'

She cursed at herself — but her legs remained locked, the phone may as well have been on Mars and not four feet over the bed. She remembered the time her dog had died. She was only ten. She had gone to bed for days, doing nothing except eating toast and getting up for the toilet. Her mother had been indulgent then, but there was no disguising that she was disappointed in her daughter's lack of resilience.

'Shut up. Shut up,' she screamed, and tore the tele-phone right out of the wall. It came away easily. She looked at the frail wires that had been rooted in her wall for years, they looked curiously like the shoots growing out of cellar potatoes. Perhaps all these distinctions between animate, inanimate were arbitrary anyway. The telephone was dead. The gloss on the receiver dimmed.

She must dress. She must get dressed and pack,

efficiently, her one holdall. One by one she looked at her tweed skirts. They had been bought to bolster her sense of respectability and solidity, instead they had swum about her waist like muddy water. Ashling had a way of looking at her in them. Is it unusual, she wondered, going to rest her head against the wet window, to wilt under the critical eye of your own child.

'You look like a middle aged trump,' she said, and thought of the jogging suits that the mothers of Ashling's friends wore.

Her fingers were so numb with cold it was hard to dress herself. The buttons on the blouse were so difficult, the trousers so bulky and the weight of the jumper unnatural. She giggled with the effort and was afraid of someone getting impatient with her. Thank God there' were boots, thank God for the lack of laces.

Dressed, she stood at the window, her hands pressed into her armpits. There were trees like scoops of cabbage all the way up the mountains. Not that they looked like mountains in comparison to the ones in last year's calendar that she'd kept in a kitchen drawer. Still, the view was something to look at, she supposed, even if it was like old scrag-end in comparison to the Alps for instance. She just wondered what people saw in it, why the rapture. What was so natural about nature? She didn't feel that she would miss it at all. It would be easy just to stand here, like this, doing nothing until next week, next spring, however long she was allowed.

'I'll need at least one complete change of clothes.' She moved away from the window, the cold was making her head ache, 'I'll need three blouses, two jumpers, two more trousers, some of Billy's socks for the warmth.' She carried on talking, finding the composing of lists, as always, a comfort.

But when at last she began to pack she did so hurriedly, jamming articles down into the holdall, letting the rest of her clothes fall where they would, trampling on them in her haste to get the bag filled and zipped. It was possible that air was slowly bleeding out of the double-glazed windows, that she would find herself gasping in a vacuum. Perhaps that wasn't true but unless she hurried she would get nothing done. In the corridor it was better, the air rushed in and out of her lungs.

The best thing to do would be to go to the lounge, sit quietly for a few minutes, think, and then make plans. Instead she found herself, holdall in hand, walking in and out of all the rooms in the house. That was unusual in itself, normally she went from one place to another to fetch something, to carry something. Now as she went round the house she felt the boredom of a visitor examining the exhibits in a museum. The kind of place where, despite all the curator's efforts, the past boils down to broken pots and old bones. She looked at the vinyl work-surfaces, the almost-wood presses, armchairs with head-rests. It was a construct, an exhibit, it was impossible to picture the people who would walk in these rooms, to conjure up the conversations they would have.

'Good evening.'

'Good evening, did you have a good day?'

'My day at work was enjoyable. It was successful.'

'Yes?'

'Yes. Today I sold three central-heating systems to customers.'

'That is good news.'

'Yes. Soon we will be able to afford that holiday in Spain.'

'Yes.'

They have museums like that now, exact replicas of neolithic campsites or Louis XIV drawing-rooms and when you press a button the tapes start up. She opened and closed the lounge door but there was no sound-track, just silence. There was nobody else, no visitors. If the aliens came here she could give them a guided tour. She saw herself throwing open doors, chattering on as they peered with serious attention at the bathroom and the device for heating food in the kitchen. They would cluster ponderously around her as she demonstrated the tech-niques used in ironing a normal wash, shaking their heads in disapproval or amazement. One by one they would begin drifting away from her excited commentary. She would find herself running from room to room trying to stop them dissecting armchairs, squeezing obscene blue trails of toothpaste, dismantling everything in the search for a meaningful relic. Finally backed against the hot press, she would see them turn to her and, recognising the greed in their faces, she would open her mouth very wide and scream.

'Billy, Billy,' she muttered, not hearing herself. Automatically she went over and turned on the television. There was a programme about tropical fish. A bland fat man bubbled happily about temperature and correct diet. What kind of foolishness, she thought, showing programmes like this in a time of national emergency. It was typical of them, getting everyone distracted with worry and then trying to calm them down with a programme on golden carp. She wasn't supposed to be using electricity, but two wrongs do not make a right.

Bending back up from unplugging the set, her eye was caught by the wedding photograph on top of the television. There was Billy's face, breaking with laughter, there were his brown eyes, his curly hair, and there she was, hanging on his arm, seeming to smile reluctantly, but that was only the contrast. She thought of the time she'd told him she was pregnant and how he insisted on ringing everyone in their phonebook with the news.

She was glad to think that he'd be alright. Ashling would be alright as well, and she could look after Eoin. Colette loved Eoin, he was easy to love. He was too young to criticise or to be the measure of her own self-criticism. She felt her hand against her throat. It was odd to think they had been nine months in her body and had come out intact. Gently she picked up the wedding photograph and the one of the children in the back garden and hid them in the waste-paper basket. No one would look for them there. They would be safe.

'I must eat,' she said. 'I need to eat. It would be good to have something to eat.'

There were plenty of tins in the press but somehow she hadn't the heart to use a tin opener. Besides most of that stuff needed heating and the cooker was cut off. At this stage opening the fridge door would cause a catastrophe so she must choose something from the table. She looked, but the potatoes didn't appeal to her, nor the carrots, onions or turnips. At least the meat hasn't been floured, she thought as she slid a piece along her tongue. In fact it was very like her tongue, like a spare tongue. She took care not to chew but to suck it slowly.

Everything was disconnected, all the windows were shut and the batteries in the radio would give out sooner or later. The house was ready and empty. Perhaps refugee families would camp here, building small fires on the kitchen carpet, huddled together against the cold and the fear. Who could guess what they had fled from, what had brought them here. A child might start crying but would be silenced by panic-stricken arms. They would talk in whispers, breaking off uneasily, listening for the sounds of pursuit. Colette pitied them also. She pitied their thin bodies and their timidity.

'I can't stay here,' she said at last. She repeated the sentence: 'I can't stay here.'

The road maps were in the car with Billy. In the bookcase was a large world Atlas stiff with countries David Attenborough had visited, but it was too heavy to carry. She must go without it. It would be a long walk, miles and miles, with little chance of ever getting home again. She took her coat from the peg and put it on. She could take the keys with her or leave them, just as she liked. Carefully she lifted the raw colourless strip of meat out of her mouth and laid it to rest in the ashtray. She picked up the holdall. She stood in front of the door, swaying slightly on the back of her heels. She was waiting for her courage to come.

On the Wall

Hand in hand Mary and Maeve Seagrove walked down the steps to the basement flat at 28 Hall Road. The leaves of the dark hedge were filmed in dust, a soapy dust that had burst unevenly all down the passageway. Water gushed hot and loud from the drainpipe to the open drain.

'Great,' said Mary and kicked the door. 'Another bloody palace.'

'Let's go in, ' said Maeve. 'Let's see first.'

'What do you need to see? Have you no imagination? We'd be better off sleeping on the Embankment, or under the Westway. Jesus Christ, can you smell that drain?'' She put the key in the lock and gave it a vicious wringing turn.

The air that greeted them was musty and damp. There was furniture everywhere, a herd of wooden and woebegone creatures who'd lumbered into the flat and had died there blocking all the windows.

'The windows are very dirty,' said Maeve.

'And what about these curtains?' asked Mary, holding a handful of material. 'Tell me honestly what colour do you think these curtains are?'

'Purple,' said Maeve. 'Let's explore properly.'

They wandered separately from room to room, calling out comments to one another. Finally they sat down at either end of a draped sofa in the living-room. Mary rolled a cigarette and lit it, the signal for serious conversation.

'You first,' said Mary.

'Well, there is a bit of a garden, sort of, and a shed. '

'A convenient place for every cat in the country to come and piss in. Great.'

'The rooms are a good size.'

'Good for what? A good size for what?'

'I don't know. Parties I suppose.'

'You don't like parties.'

'You do,' said Maeve.

Mary got up and began moving restlessly round the room. 'Somebody's died in here, I bet you. You can feel it. Some poor old lady. Of bloody hypothermia.' She shivered.

'We could paint it. We could paint it with lots of bright colours. It wouldn't look the same.'

'Anything to get out of that squat, eh?' said Mary kindly.

'They don't like me.'

'Ah now.'

'You know they don't.'

Mary bent down and kissed her on the forehead. 'It's not personal you know.'

Maeve shrugged and looked away. 'Maybe it'd look better if we took off these filthy old dust sheets. ' Cautiously she lifted the corner of one that covered a colossal armchair then dropped the sheet back. 'I have never seen such an ugly object in my life,' she said triumphantly.

Down the road at The Winchester their prospective landlord was breaking the filter off a Silk Cut cigarette. If he noticed them coming in he gave no sign. Mary sat down sideways in the chair, she always used her profile when nervous.

'It's a kip,' she began.

The man pursed his lips thoughtfully.

'And you're asking too much.' There was a clatter and the key with its cardboard ticket lay between them.

'It's your choice,' he said agreeably, not picking up the key.

Maeve was looking at the bronze, brown and clear liquids that dazzled in bottles behind the bar. She loved the way the glass pushed up the silver nozzle and made the liquid pour. The barman caught her eye in the mirror and winked at her. She looked away.

'You must think I'm drunk or daft,' snorted Mary.

The landlord was rolling his cigarette clockwise, very gently between his forefinger and thumb. His fingers were the same colour as his signet ring. 'As I said, it's entirely up to you Mrs. . .' He hesitated the barest moment.

'I'm not married.'

Maeve watched the man's other hand lift up from the table and tug at the long lobe of an ear. He was smiling.

'It does need a lick of paint,' he admitted, and finally lit his cigarette. 'I tell you what, my dear, how would it be if I let you off a week's rent, no let's make it two. Two weeks rent-free.'

'Month,' said Maeve.

'Two weeks,'' said their landlord calmly. ''You'll both have a drink with me I hope, to settle the business.''

'I'll want a proper rent book.'

'Ask and you shall receive. Gin and tonic do. you, and an orange juice for the little lady?'

'I'll have a Pepsi Cola,' said Maeve, 'and my mother drinks whiskey.''

Clearing out their things from the squat was a slow resentful procedure. Steve's new girlfriend trailed after to make sure they didn't accidentally walk off with anything that wasn't theirs. Maeve sat on the stairs, listening to the arguments, the most bitter over a red mixing bowl. Mary claiming it was definitely hers, the girlfriend that it was Steve's. Maeve could have told them it really belonged to Janice. She didn't because she knew it would do no good.

'We should tell Grandma we moved,' said Maeve.

'Damn right we should.'

'We should, ' insisted Maeve.

'And we'll have to fix up a nice school for you of course,' Mary said in her faraway voice. 'I'll bet there are lots of really nice schools just round the corner.'

Maeve said nothing, there was a limit to pushing Mary. She wouldn't mention Grandma again.

'What in the name of God will we do with all this junk?' Mary looked despairingly on the massed ranks of oak and mahogany. She paused. 'We'll have to drag whatever we can into the garden and set fire to it there. '

'Won't it kill the grass?'

Streams of dust rose from the discarded sheets, flakes of newspaper scattered over the undistinguished carpet. Chairs with burst bottoms, cracked lampshades, gritty mats and a mouse-eaten mattress were the first things to go. Slowly they walked out a solemn old chest of drawers, a table, a box of books, until the pile was halfway between the height of Mary and Maeve.

'Have a last check round,' Mary called as Maeve ran back into the flat.

In the shed Mary found a rusty can half filled with something that smelt like petrol. She splashed it all over the heap, pouring it in great satisfying glugs into the heart of the mattress. 'It's going to burn, Christ, it's going to burn,' she hummed excitedly. 'Come on Maeve, where are you?'

'I'm here,' said a clear voice.

'You can't be here because I'm here and I can't see you at all.'

'Don't be silly, I'm in the lounge.'

'The lounge, the lounge,' sighed Mary. 'Now where would an innocent child pick up an expression like lounge?'

Maeve was flushed with the effort of trying to tug something from behind the sofa. Her nose wrinkled up at the smell on Mary's hands. 'It's trapped,' she said.

'What is it?' said Mary, and untangled a carved

corner from the material at the back of the sofa. 'A picture is it?'

It wasn't a picture, it was a mottled and ugly looking mirror set squarely in an over-ornamented piece of walnut. Mary wiped it with the sleeve of her work shirt but only a dingy sheen broke over the glass surface and their faces were poorly reflected in the decoloured depths. A set of hooks had been screwed in the bottom of the frame.

'What are these for I wonder?' asked Mary. "For hats or for hanging mice?'

'I don't know.'

'We'll have to get a cat you know,' Mary leant the mirror against the body of the sofa. 'It's got more freckles than both of us put together. OK I'll lift it out and we can start the bonfire.'

'Don't let's,' pleaded Maeve. 'Don't let's burn it.'

'It's not bad luck to burn mirrors only to break them.'

'Look.' Maeve pointed out a half-clean patch on the wall paper in front of them. 'That's where it comes from. Besides there isn't any other mirror anywhere, I've looked.'

'It'll be too high up for you.'

'I'll stand on the sofa then.'

Maeve took Mary's hand and they went out into the garden.

The fire flashed noisily into life the moment Mary set a match to it. The flames seemed higher than the house and the heat haze made the sky pucker and wilt. It was too large a fire for such a small place, smoke choked them and Maeve was very nearly frightened. It was difficult to see anything, even each other, just glimpses between the fume of yellow smoke and the colourless twists of flame. But when the fire burnt back eventually, half the heap of rubbish was still there, thoroughly changed and blackened. It hadn't been so powerful after all. Mary kicked a lump of wood and a weary puff of grey dust and smoke rose up.

'We'd better go to the Soc, then,' she said. 'Before it closes. Come on and wash your face.'

In the waiting-room they shifted slowly from chair to chair. The first time Maeve had played musical chairs was at a party, she disliked parties and she disliked this place. There were newspapers here and there, limp from use and with all the crosswords completed. A small child in a red furry all-in-one suit counted cigarette butts under his mother's chair. His nose was running, there was a thin crust of matter on his upper lip.

'Seagrove cubicle seventeen,' came an exhausted voice through the microphone.

The woman behind the counter was thirty years old, her face was brown and divided up inch by inch by the green wire embedded in the glass. Mary was talking.

'It's a change of address that's all, no change in circumstances. I haven't married, had more kids, got a job.'

'I'd be grateful if you could just fill in the forms, that's all I want you to do,' said the woman. She was wearing a pink sari and a pink cardigan. Maeve couldn't decide which pink was the wrong pink but one of them was.

'I'm telling you now,' said Mary, ignoring the last remarks, 'none of your bloody delaying tactics — I want my money and I want it by Thursday.'

'Your address is secure? There's no one sharing with you?' The woman sounded tired and polite.

'Why don't you send someone round to check,' sneered Mary.

'You will get a visitor in due course.' The woman blinked very slowly. Maeve copied her and saw the whole world crushed into one black line. She doesn't like Mary, Maeve realised. 'And you will have your giro on your doormat on Thursday.'

The giro was there on Thursday but not on the doormat. They hadn't a doormat. Some of the money went on food, some on paint. On the way back from the supermarket Mary phoned Sally and told her to come round that afternoon to begin painting. They both agreed that Sally was very trying but she was also very obliging.

'We won't bother stripping the walls,' Mary began when they were all assembled. 'We'll just slap the paint up as it is.'

'Did I tell you what Mark and I did last week,' Sally said her eyes wide open.

'I'll go and play in the garden,' said Maeve, and went out.

She walked round the unburnt bonfire and over to the shed. The heat had raised some very interesting blisters on the door, they were like scabs or skinny milk. Maeve ran her finger then her tongue along one of them. She liked them for the same reason she liked cracked mud and dead motorcars.

'Hello,' she whispered to the door.

Steadily she chipped and picked little green half-moons of paint off the wood. It would take time to free this door, perhaps months. She would clear a small square every day, saving the hinges until last. The wood underneath was splintery and too wet to be brown or any other colour. It always delighted her to watch something change, to be the one to make it change. When she'd finished maybe the door wouldn't open into the shed at all. She longed always to find the opening, the passageway into that other world. She was thinking this and balancing a wrinkled strip of paint on the back of her hand, not allowing the wind to blow it away.

'Look at your runners,' said Mary when she came in. Maeve looked at them. 'Take the bloody things off. Sally's made us a nice vegetable stew.' Sally popped her head round the kitchen door, still smiling. 'So eat it.'

'I like your cooking best,' said Maeve loyally.

'Creep,' said Mary, and Maeve blushed.

Sally came in carrying two slopping bowls of stew, one for Maeve at the table and one she left on a chair near where Mary was lying stretched out on the sofa flicking an extinct cigarette against the side of an ashtray.

'Well, what do you think of the wall Mary painted? '

asked Sally, bringing in her own bowl.

'She thinks it's bloody marvellous, don't you?' said Mary, rotating her left foot, then her right foot, ignoring the stew. "What a life, what a total . . .'

'Don't,' said Sally.

Maeve was moving the uncooked carrots in a neat ring round the rim of her bowl, five slices so far. The beans were hard as well. 'I'm going out tonight,' said Mary, 'I'm going out and getting totally legless. OK?'

In her bathroom Mary sat on the side of the bath watching Maeve brush her teeth. "You're too young to be left without a babysitter. Supposing you woke up and you're frightened. Do you remember where The Winchester is even?'

Maeve inclined her head, her mouth full of foaming spittle.

Mary stroked her hair. 'You look tired, you'll sleep well. It'll be weeks before this dump is liveable in.'

'I hoovered your bedroom and mine you know,' said Maeve. "Twice.'

'Mother's little helper,' said Mary and grimaced, then laughed.

The bedroom was small and quiet. The crack of light from the doorway fanned out over the floor. She could see flying bits of grey in the high corners. They moved, just a little. Mary and Sally were in the corridor, one voice quick and impatient the other smudged.

'Goodnight,' they called out and the front door slammed behind them.

She lay without breathing to the count of fifty but nobody came back. To be on the safe side she recounted all the numbers before deciding it was alright to slide out and explore. The flat was very cold so she put on the Mickey Mouse slippers that Mary had bought her for Christmas.

The light-switch in the hall was hidden behind a branching pole of clothes but Maeve found it and turned the light out.

Immediately the lino in the hallway was darker and

longer, it even looked wet. In the lounge the new wall glowed white and smelt of paraffin. It was pleasant to stick and unstick her fingers on that fresh surface. She was in a box of shadows that flickered with the branches of outside trees and the bars across the windows. The light here didn't come from the sun or from a switch, it was a natural quality that all objects left in peace radiated. It was everywhere, it was indiscriminate and even her slippers, if she had glanced at them, would have seemed, would have been, transformed.

She glided round the room, touching old satin and hard wood, everything was colder than cold. She danced a little and sang under her breath to show that she was here and ready. Now she must do something, she must find some way to push herself past the last bit of familiarity and over the bearable edge. That was the hardest thing and only rarely had she approached the brink of that moment when the whole world changed. She lifted her arms at angles from her body and fixed one foot to the floor while the other pushed against the carpet. She began to whirl. Hair spun round her, nonsense syllables spilled breathlessly out of her mouth, and still she went faster. The windows went by so quick they were disappearing and faster still she beat her foot against the floor. It was a race now but the sickness was winning, coming up to her throat, and soon she could not contain it. Then she was lying in the lap of the sofa, dizzy, panting like a dog for air. She had failed, she felt hot and stiff with shame and the room wore a sarcastic expression on its face. She ran back to bed.

Next morning Mary asked, 'How am I supposed to eat toast without butter, or margarine or something to spread?' She stabbed the empty tub with her knife.

'I could go to the shops,' said Maeve from the bathroom.

'No point unless you can shop-lift,' replied Mary. 'I should have got some yesterday while we still had money.' She paused. 'I could teach you to lift stuff I suppose, but you're bound to get caught. You've that sort of face. Like mine. They'd put you in care and call me an unfit mother. I'm not an unfit mother, just unfit. Isn't that right?'

Maeve came into the living-room. 'Are we broke so soon?'

'Have some tea,' advised Mary, 'and I saved you a banana.'

Maeve had sat down in her chair before she noticed anything unusual. Quickly she hid her nose under the rim of her mug and so disguised could stare without seeming to at the carpet. What was there? Long, semi-shining lines, not silver but possessing last night's midnight uncoloured light. It could be a sign, it could be a message traced out for her alone to see.

'What do you want to do today,' asked Mary ' because I'm not doing any more bloody housework. '

· 'I don't mind.'

Mary got up, tea pot in hand, and walked over to the kitchen. It was clear that whatever was on the carpet was invisible to Mary. Her feet made no impression on it. Maeve's lungs hardened with all the air that was in them but she knew better than to shout with excitement. Here was a secret she must not share.

In the afternoon Maeve cleaned the bathroom while Mary worked on the cooker. It helped Mary if Maeve did things, it encouraged her. It was important to get the place clean and comfortable because Mary, who was restless, might want to stay then. Maeve watched the water swirl round and round the plughole for as long as the tap was turned on. In the centre was a hole the size of the round O her finger and thumb made when joined together.

Just as she was crossing the threshold of the living-room, her cleaner and cloth in hand, she caught sight of the mirror. Then, immediately, she knew the place where her creatures hid during the daylight hours. What else possessed that exact shade of translucence when not covered and camouflaged with a mirage of reflections. It was a disguise so magical, so variable that no hint was given of what lay hidden inside. Almost without thinking she climbed up the sofa arm to stare down into its depths. If she was quick maybe she would see the effervescent astonishing . . . but Maeve was only looking at Maeve. She dared the reflection to blink before she did.

Mary laughed. 'Look how you've grown, you're taller than me." She turned Maeve's hands between her own and blew on them with her warm breath. 'Christ you're cold. This flat's an icebox.'

'How's the cooker?' asked Maeve. 'Did you get it clean?'

'I'm not cut out to be a housewife.' Mary moved over to the table and her tobacco pouch. 'You can't really like this place you know.'

'I love it,' said Maeve.

'Why?' asked Mary. 'Wouldn't you rather be at Grandma's with all that lovely central heating, lovely dinners and lovely —'

'No.'

That night and the next Maeve slept on and on through dreams until daylight and woke up furious with herself for having missed them in the night. In the bathroom her gums bled and she could see that her hair was greasy. She was tired now and sitting on the sofa she stared almost listlessly at the long wavering silver lines on the carpet.

'Guess what's for breakfast,' called out Mary. 'It's pancakes, pancakes and more pancakes. With maple syrup and cream.'

'Great.'

Mary entered a plate in either hand, she was happy. ' We got another giro today.' She blew a kiss in the direction of Notting Hill DHSS.

'But —'

'That was only an emergency payment but this is our real one. Have you ever known them that quick? Isn't it great? Eat this while it's hot.'

That afternoon Mary went up to the market but Maeve said she didn't want to go. First she went out to the shed and picked another few square inches of paint from the shed door, but that was too easy. The burnt bed springs she had snapped before, and nothing else was interesting. In the end she went to the sofa and climbed up. There was a kind of excitement in her stomach but the crossing and uncrossing of her eyes produced no effect. Mary would certainly go out this evening and there was more chance of them appearing if she was alone in the flat.

At ten o'clock she was tucked up and lying there drifting in and out of sleep like a ship at anchor. Then gradually out of the creaking quiet of the flat a sound of the soft splashing and lapping of liquids began to come clear. It was only after a while that she realised she was hearing the sound of them sliding through the skin of the mirror and onto the floor next door. Each individual arrived with a curious musical echo, more audible than anything ordinary could be. Her skin began to tingle and her fingers to drum in rhythm with the sound. It wasn't the weight of the blankets or the warmth of the bed that held her there but a sudden sense of how different they might be. For the first time she was afraid. Perhaps these creatures didn't like strangers, and they might find her very strange indeed. Violently she pressed one ear against the pillow and wished they lived in another house.

The week began to go past. On Friday the landlord called round for his rent and offered to take Mary down for a drink in The Winchester if she fancied. She said she wasn't in the mood and nobody sat down during his visit. A few of Mary's friends had found out where she was living and began to call round.

There'd be parties soon, all-night affairs and people would sleep in the living-room if they were too tired to go home. That would keep the beautiful creatures shut away behind the mirror. Maeve wasn't sure whether to be glad or sorry about that.

'You'll have to go to school soon,' said Mary.

'I don't want to.'

'We all have to do things we don't want to do. I'll get into trouble if you don't.'

'Why?'

'Don't be stupid, Maeve.' Mary picked up a book that someone had left behind and yawned just the way she did when Sally bored her. 'You know the score.'

'You don't. Why should I, if you don't.'

Mary smiled and began reading her book as though everything had been agreed and settled. There was nothing Maeve knew to say or to do, she sat and tapped her foot against the table leg. She thought of going to her room, or going to the shed door to pick at the paint but somehow couldn't leave the room. There was nothing on the mirror but a blank expanse of whitened wallpaper.

The doorbell rang. Mary threw the book across the room and got up. 'Who in hell is that?' she asked and went to answer it.

The book had landed on an armchair. Maeve picked it up to pretend that she was absorbed in reading.

'Well,' came Mary's exclaiming voice through the doorway, 'well will you guess who it is?'

A tall man with a packed brown briefcase stood in the doorway, his sheepskin jacket swinging open. Clearly he was not a friend from the way he looked round the room and back to Maeve.

'It's Mr Baker from the DHSS. Give the gentleman a big smile won't you?'

Maeve gave him a look, not hostile, as he wasn't a school inspector. Without wasting any time he sat down and surreptitiously patted his nose with his gloves before taking them off. 'Let's keep this brief, shall we?'

'Don't mind us, we've nothing else to do.' Mary moved all the things that were on the table and crammed them down the end furthest away from Mr Baker. He took out a file without comment.

'So, Mrs Seagrove —'

'I'm not married,' said Mary triumphantly.

'I'm sorry.'

'I'm not.'

'No I meant . . .' he regained control 'and this I take it is your daughter?'

'I'm Maeve.'

'She's home from school with a cold,' announced Mary. Maeve sniffed. 'Go and get a handkerchief.'

She got two squares of toilet tissue and waited until she was back in the room before blowing her nose. It was obvious that Mr Baker wanted to blow his nose as well but was not in a position to ask for a tissue. Every now and again he would lift his glove as if absently and touch the tip of his nose with it.

'So you live alone then, you live alone apart from Maeve here.' He tapped the biro against the file.

'Why don't you search the place?' suggested Mary.

'I'd be obliged if you could just answer me in a civil fashion.'

Maeve could see that the muscles on his face were flat and tight already.

'And I'd appreciate being treated in one,' said Mary.

'There are regulations concerning cohabiting.' Mary raised an eyebrow in mock surprise. He continued, 'as I am sure you are aware. As I hope you are also aware, it is an offence to give false information when submitting a claim to the Department.'

'There's just us living here.'

'Thank you.' He cleared his neck from his collar and wrote something down.

'Would you like a cup of tea?' asked Mary.

'No, thank you.'

'You don't mind if I smoke do you?' said Mary anxiously. 'They're only very small cigarettes.' She showed him one rolled up like a matchstick.

'I don't myself,' he said, and made a gesture permitting her to light up.

She did and suddenly smiled at him. 'Christ I bet that coat's lovely and warm.'

'It's very shabby I'm afraid, now if we could —'

'But warm, doesn't it look warm Maeve? Come here Maeve.' Mary lifted one of Maeve's hands and waved it at Mr Baker. 'Her hands are like blocks of ice. The sheets she sleeps in are damp with cold. Is it any wonder she has bronchitis? The old lady who lived here before us died of bloody hypothermia, did you know that?'

'There is, calculated in your overall entitlement, a specific allowance for both heat and light.'

'It's not enough.'

'You can make a special needs application but frankly —'

'There's fungus in the kitchen. One wall is completely covered in it. Come and see for yourself. Isn't there any regulations about cohabiting with fungus?' High on adrenalin Mary gripped the table and dared Mr Baker to avert his gaze. He continued to regard her with a look of settled weariness.

'I'm sure you realise Ms Seagrove —' he didn't seem to mind when she interrupted him again.

'And what about this.' She was on her feet and pointing down. 'What do you suppose that is on the carpet?'

There was total silence, absolute zero in the room. Maeve's mouth was dry and in her chest was a thumping like someone methodically beating down a door. She kept her eyes fixed on the round bumps of her knees but she could see and feel Mary rushing across the room and over to the sofa.

'Look,' commanded Mary. Lockjawed Mr Baker and mesmerised Maeve in synchronisation turned their heads and saw Mary straining with all of her strength to pull the sofa onto its back.

Its stubby little legs were helplessly exposed, but there was something else to see. There, underneath, clinging to the open-weave canvas Maeve saw curled-up scraps of pinkish grey flesh. They were soft like tongues, curled like thumbs, and all of them pulsed, pulsed to some slow nearly extinct rhythm.

The adults were talking. 'Well —?'

'As I've said —'

'As you've said.'

'You don't appreciate —'

'Appreciate what? Appreciate having slugs in my

front room?'

Maeve didn't move, she was standing still but not too near them, her eyes fixed and her lips loosely working. She watched the blunt-branched movement of their heads and knew to an exactitude how cool and sticky they would be to the touch. She would not touch them. She knew of what kind and quality they were. Who knew how many more were hidden away in the open hole of the mirror above their heads?

The man had disappeared, there was only Mary in the room, silent at first, but then talking, exulted, reliving her repartee. Lack of success always enlivened her. She was recalling other caustic remarks and cunning stories of the past that had nevertheless led nowhere. She was even trying to turn the sofa back on its right side, but without the fury she lacked the strength. She was cursing now.

'Why don't you help me? What are you staring at? Give us a hand. What are you staring at?' Mary shouted.

'Nothing,' said Maeve.

The Enchantment

The man was sleeping, back and forwards he swayed with the movement of the horse. All around stretched the open plain. There was no sound, just wave after wave of grass rustling against his feet. From sky to sky there was nothing except the man, the horse and the round red sun.

The last loop of the reins he had long relinquished. The horse's head was free, but it was too weary even to halt. Up and down thumped the hooves like an engine — like an engine, past hunger, past thirst. The sweat of both soaked the saddle and their breath came equally hard and ragged. The man was talking in his sleep. He was pleading. It was the sound of that voice that woke him.

There was nothing to see except the things he had seen already. He was adrift in this mad dry ocean without land or stars to guide him. The only patterns were ones the wind made moving through the grass; there, then gone.

'Halt,' he whispered to the horse. I must pull on the reins, he thought, that is what I must do. 'Halt,' his voice croaked and he tried feebly to catch at one of the reins. His hand wasn't quick enough, it couldn't grip. There wasn't water enough in his body for him to weep.

On and on the horse stumbled like a motor refusing to die. Die, thought the man, for the love of God, lie down and die. Let us both lie down here, anywhere here, and rest. We have suffered enough. There is no need for this. Death would pass through and be barely noticed. The man looked down the infinite distance to the ground. He leant his head over the horse's shoulder and toppled down with a jarring crash of metal. The horse's legs buckled. It stood one second, two, before dropping down into the grass.

Man and horse slept.

Sounds of rain woke him, bringing a refreshment that was almost pain. Half-asleep, he sucked at the wet grass. It washed over his face, over his armour. Harder it came, like hailstones, hopping from his shoulders in notes of music. His hands tore convulsively at the grass. He could not stand against the breaking weight of the water, he crawled to the brown mound of horse on his left.

'Horse,' he whispered. 'Horse.'

He saw rain brimming in the open eye of the animal, the chest exposed like a dead drum. Its teeth, like the moon, were yellow and enormous. He put grass in its mouth for a farewell. It was puzzling that he could not remember his companion's name. He sighed. He knew it deserved praise, it had carried him far and here it had died like an animal.

' Iron heart, ' he murmured. 'Old Ironheart.'

Round to the back of the beast he crawled, the mud oozing into the joints of his armour. How useless and stiff his fingers were, how he cursed at them, but at last both saddle-bag and sword were free. He patted the bag affectionately and used the sword to help him stand. He looked down at the horse for a moment but there was nothing there to eat, just skin and bone. He kicked it and in a last reflex one of its legs skittered a few feet across the mud.

Indiscriminate water was everywhere, he was ankle

deep in mud already. If he did not move, he would not be able to move. He walked, mud splattering up to his waist and the rain rinsing it off. Without the help of the sword to steady him he would have slipped and perhaps drowned in the sodden earth. He had no purpose, only the habit of survival.

He awoke next morning with light, indelicately bright, breaking through the branches and burning his eyelids. His face felt hot and foolish and he sat up groaning. It was fiercely warm. Steam rose from the tree moss, at first light so saturated with water as to be black, by now green, and at nightfall it would be a brittle shadow just yellow on the tree bark. Overhead a flight of birds shook out over the forest. He blinked but everything stayed clear. His lips were cracked and his tongue so shrivelled that it could not reach the roof of his mouth. To the left of him was the sound of a stream and that was more astonishing, more delightful, than any escape from the open plain.

Speechless he made his way to the creek and tore handful after handful of water up to his mouth. Then he plunged his face open-eyed under the surface to soothe his sore and dirty skin. Feeling human, like a man again, he unbuckled each piece of armour and laid it to one side. His tunic and trousers would need washing, it was strange to consider the quantity of filth his body could create. Down the creek he slid and let the cool water cover him like a second skin. With one hand against the bank to steady him he stared down into the calm still pool of the sun. His body seemed to float under the influence of that gentle light. His eyes widened, water trickled over his head into his mouth . . .

He pulled himself gasping back on the bank. He stayed there half blinded and kneeling. He looked down at his arm, it was pink and bald, all his body was pink and bald. There were lesions and welts on his back, his shoulders, raw places that bled. The water had tried to take him and change him. He was afraid. As fast as he could he hid himself inside the armour, keeping his face both set and angry.

' I must not be tempted. '

Breakfast was a handful of wormy nuts. It took him careful hours to catch two very small fish. One he ate immediately and the other he hung to dry on a willow tree. Hungry though he was it was hard to stomach raw fish, but he had long ago lost the flint to make a fire. He must eat his food raw or wind dried. He leant his back against the tree. The fish quivered in the breeze above him.

He took the jar of grease and rags from his saddle-bag and began to clean those parts of his armour accessible to his reach. The gauntlets, finger by finger, the wrist plates, the broad disk of the chestplate and the articulated legs were scraped and greased and polished. It was a soothing and relaxing process. He knew it was important to take account of appearances. He took particular care of the helmet, with its intricate hinges, flaps and decorations. There was nothing to be done about the back of the armour, it must stay stained and rusted. When he tried to scratch up against the trunk of a tree flakes of rust did float down, but his own body was too tender for such treatment.

The shadow of the leaves flickered over his gleaming body. A fat-bodied butterfly, bristle-black between two gold-and-purple wings, seemed about to settle, then wavering flew away. He sighed, stood up. The jar and the rags he packed back into the bag. He had little enough left — the broken half of a dagger and a box of salt, a bag of coins that could buy nothing here. Still, he was reluctant to lose anything. He hoisted the bag over one shoulder, the sword over the other and, turning, leapt over the brook.

The air under the trees of the forest was wet and cool. A man could walk many hours without discomfort, he thought. The sun was broken up and scattered by the branches and had lost its strength. He liked the tall succession of tree after tree, all individuals no doubt but indistinguishable. Undergrowth cracked under his feet and he liked that sound, for there was always the danger of loneliness.

'You must mark the trees,' a voice said. 'You must mark a path for yourself.'

Perhaps it was a pity he had not been told to do that before. The creek was many minutes behind him now and who could tell in which direction it lay. The best trees for his purpose were the white trunked birches that were bruised already with many dark discolourations. One after another he notched with swings of his sword, some he killed altogether, but they were only saplings and too thin anyway. There were always more standing out in semi-phosphorescence against the dark undergrowth. Panting, he harried and hunted them, pounding down brambles, almost running despite the weight of his armour. Sweat poured all over him and there were always more and more to tantalise him onward. The time came when he had to stop, dizzy with fatigue. He had to unlace his helmet. As the sound of his breathing subsided he heard high above him the chattering of a squirrel. There it rode on the frailest branches, dipping into the air, bobbling like a bead of blood before the eyes. It was not concerned with him.

He began trudging back along the wild, random path he had carved out. There was a chance that at the end of it he could intuit a way back to the river. He wanted something familiar. He thought of his beautiful succulent fish. He looked all about him. He had been mad to leave such traces of his progress as these trees that called to any enemy, come find me. He cursed the man who had given him such advice. Now he must hide away in the undergrowth and plan the future.

A grey and startled mammal flashed between his feet. He pierced it neatly though the backbone, surprised himself at the speed of his reaction. He hugged himself approvingly and ate. Ants crawled up the stems of the grass all around him. There must be thousands upon millions simmering on the floor of the forest. He licked one off his gauntlet, its taste was insubstantial.

' You have come far,' a voice jeered at him.

It was easy to conceal the bones and skin in the friable earth between the roots of a tree. He did it quickly because he knew that he had no time to waste. When he stood up he realised that his saddle-bag had gone. It had been lost or stolen, or it had vanished. It would have been good to know which.

At any moment he would decide whether to turn back or to struggle down deeper into the forest. Even bare, even without his helmet, his head was buzzing. It was as hard to imagine a future as it was to remember the past. The more time he remained the more fixed he would become, like a fly in amber. The leaves shivered overhead. There was a bird in the clearing and on its tiny bill a beetle the size of a thumb joint reflexively writhed. In one movement the bird tossed its throat open and swallowed. Then, without seeming to open its wings, it shot into the air. He was sorry to see it go. It was so bright and lively, with kindness he could have tamed it. There would be tales told of the knight and the nightingale, if it was a nightingale.

' Come, ' he said gently, and went.

There were no paths or trackways, even the beasts left little sign of their passage. He knew better now than to mark his own way and kept his sword balanced over his shoulder. To travel he would pick a landmark, a stump, a tree, a bush, and march steadily towards it. Once there he would pick another and go to that. This he would do until nightfall. At nightfall he would lie down and sleep. The plan was clear and he would obey it. Soon he would get to the centre of the wood, there was even hope that he would get to the other side. He believed that there was a centre and that there was another side.

And what could be more pleasant than to ramble through these broadleafed woods? He walked with his head high and the helmet secured by leather thongs to his waist. He liked the sound of it clattering in a companionable way at his side. Occasionally he would pat its head, but he did that absently. The late afternoon sun trickled like syrup through the branches and sank in hot quiescent pools all around him. There were outposts of shade and he began to dart swiftly from shadow to shadow. It began as a game, for it must be admitted that there was a certain dullness, a certain monotony, no matter how sweet the air and how good the rough red berries tasted as he snatched them running past. He kept running, his arms open, as full of flight as any bird that let the green ground tumble away beneath it. He exulted in power. He saw how the trees swayed and cowered before him, how insects immolated their frail bodies on his ironhearted armour. His voice rose like a scattering of fear and all around him things crashed and lumbered. On he ran, blinded by sweat, in a fearless panic of delight, on and on with wet flesh, jarred bones and burning blood. He would not stop, he couldn't. He would never stop.

Then he was mid-stream, on his knees, sobbing with exhaustion. All around the night had settled in and he could see very little. He took his sword and plunged the tip six inches into the ground. Before sleeping he prayed to it distractedly, all the while his ears strained for the noise of pursuit. The moon bore down. He had to rub earth and leaf-mould on his armour so that its shine could not betray him as he slept. For a while he hid in the undergrowth, then scrambled up to the fork of a tree, but there was no escape. In the end he crawled under the upturned and hairy cup of a willow tree, its straggling branches scraping together like the forelegs of an insect. He had lost the sword back there in the darkness.

Dawn came as it must and the man was woken by the overpowering smell of fish. His jaws had been working in his sleep and he was coughing on his own saliva. Here was a strange place to hide a fish, but he would not complain. He pulled open the split belly and sucked, his eyes never resting for a moment. He could hear the brook giggling to the left of him and could feel how thirsty he was. Carefully he slid his head into his helmet, for there was no sense in provocation.

With the visor down it might be possible to strain the

contents of the water before it reached his lips. This way he could make it taste of iron despite itself.

' Today ', someone urged, 'do not be tempted.'

Once over the brook it was a question of agreeing a strategy. The grass surussed against his legs. He realised he was following a path notched out among the trees. There was little sense in rejecting any assistance that was offered. From marked tree to marked tree he went, some oozing liquid as if freshly cut. There were times when he almost understood the markings and even the meaning behind the seemingly erratic pattern of the path. Above the noonday sun etched every outline of leaf and branch to a hard edge. His hands were shaking.

Abruptly the trail, if trail it was, vanished, evaporated. Far off in the forest a crashing noise and a violent outcry of birdsong. He peered through the slits of his helmet for a sign. At his feet he found the rotted remnants of some leather object. Greedily he pulled it apart and there in his hand flat discs of metal like coins of skin winked. His thumbs pricked and he felt the uncomfortable throb of his heart. He got away to a safe place and tried, there, to make sense of his situation. He left the bag and its contents where they lay, just for luck.

For a while he sat there on the tree stump uncertain of what to do. A bird, a dull brown-coloured thing, dropped suddenly out of the sky and with its bill pierced the armoured back of an insect that had the stupidity to be seen. The man got up and ran in directionless flight through trees that flickered past like the bars of a prison.

He was swimming in a sweat that burned like acid, the sour smell of rank vegetation stung his nostrils. Dark green, jade green, budding and overblown, insensate nature bloomed all about him, in the fat-lipped and glistening throats of insect-eating plants, in the rank and hyperactive fusion and confusion of tropical growth.

He lay in the stream, the coolness of the water swirled into the cracks of his armour like so many writhing snakes. He waited for the dancing fog of heat to slow, to ease and to leave him weak and exhausted where he was.

He lowered his head into the stream and drank. Through the slats of his helmet river-bed pebbles reared up like a wall against which he weakly beat his wrists. He heard the thick glottal cursing of a man made mad with fear. It babbled on and on until, at last, it ceased.

In the next dawn he woke stiff with cold and rust. He ate a handful of wormy nuts and took hours to catch two small fish. The first drops of the sun splashed on the tree-tops, where a whole colony of animals swarmed like ants. Carefully he hung the body of one fish in the recess of a tree with trailing branches. It would be safe there.

He walked forward towards the stream and in his haste stumbled across an old upright sword. Streams of birds washed overhead, crying mournfully. He watched them. At the edge of the forest he felt the sun gather up its strength. He wondered if the owner of the sword had stood as he stood now watching the trees curve and bend like the fingers of a hand beckoning with slow circular movements, calling him into the heart of a mystery he could only repeat and not penetrate.

Extravagance

It was strange that even at such a perfectly circular table she felt as though she was the one sitting in the corner. Perhaps it was wishful thinking. Jackie took a third sip from her glass.

'Typical of the bloody woman to be late for her own bloody birthday party,' said Merv, leaning the back of his head against the alcove wall. 'Too bloody typical to be true.'

'Don't start,' advised Sue.

'Start what?' drawled Merv. Then he shouted: 'Christ woman —' 'Don't call me woman.' They were clearly getting into their stride. 'What would you like me to call you?' he asked in his reasonable voice. 'That's what you are aren't you? Or were the last time I bothered to look.'

Pausing only to stretch her lips in a faint smile Sue said, 'Do you have any idea how many times you've made that particular little joke?'

'Amanda won't be long I expect,' said Ray, brightly. 'Anyway it's only half past eight.'

'It's nine,' said Gail. She lit another cigarette. She was

on a diet.

Jackie glanced at her watch, it was in fact ten to nine but there wasn't any point in saying that.

'I wonder if it's worth ordering another bottle now.' Delicately Merv lifted the empty bottle between his palms. He peered down the neck. 'Ship ahoy.'

'Where did you say you worked, Jackie?' asked Sue.

'In a law centre. In Hackney.'

'A law centre?' repeated Sue vaguely.

'That's right.'

'You a lawyer then?'

'No.'

'Ah.'

Frankly it was easier to deal with question-and-answer sessions even if they went nowhere. There was no point in trying to make conversation. Jackie knew her limitations. Across the table David was running his hand slowly over the surface of his hair. If he were a woman, she thought, he could be as vain about his hair as he liked. It was a pity really. He looked very well in his new linen suit. And if only Merv could be persuaded to order white wine next time round perhaps David would be able to relax a little more, she could see the thought of red wine stains flicker in his eyes every time a glass was raised.

Even though many of the other alcoves were full, the restaurant was quiet, its customers subdued. Unknown stringed instruments vibrated smoothly through the loudspeaker on the wall. The walls were canvas-coloured and mid-brown, from the floor reared the restrained dark wood of designer tables and designer chairs. Clearly it was going to be an expensive night, but the restaurant had been Amanda's choice and Jackie had agreed, had even asked to come. From where she was sitting she could see the Chinese waiters cover and clear the tables opposite with an almost arrogant dexterity. In a glaze of good food the Europeans watched the waiters swoop round and by them like a flock of migrant birds, some of them smiled at the waiters, amused by the cleverness, the quickness.

'What are you smiling at?' asked Merv. 'Nothing.

Those people opposite. Nothing really,' said Jackie too quickly. 'Just exercising the old facial muscles, not the same thing as smiling at all,' said Merv, looking at her from the corners of his eyes.

Ray was wondering if he'd put on weight since he last wore this suit. He was damned if he was going jogging again. 'You don't need to lose any weight,' he said to Jackie accusingly.

'I'm not.'

'Then I wouldn't bother exercising if I didn't have to. They want two hundred a year for membership at this place up the road from me,' Ray growled, then added in a deep Southern drawl, 'they want horse whipping.' It was part of his charm that his *alter ego* was a Southern gentleman from the time of the American Civil War. Anyway it made Aggie giggle, especially when they were on their own.

'Christ,' said Gail stubbing out her cigarette noisily.

There was Amanda — paused for the fleeting but memorable moment at the entrance to the alcove. She was delighted to see them all. With her hand on Aggie's shoulder she bent to kiss Ray's forehead, managing to smile over at David and Merv and with a word for Gail to apologise for her habitual lateness. She slid into the chair directly opposite Jackie. 'My God you look absolutely fabulous, Jackie,' she radiated. 'That colour. If I had those blue eyes, I'd never wear any other colour. Don't you think so Sue?'

'Is it silk?' Sue asked Jackie.

'Not exactly.' She finished her glass of wine.

The waiters gathered round the table, snapping menus in front of everyone's face.

'First things first,' said Merv, taking the wine menu from David's hand. 'Best leave it to the experts.'

'We don't know what we're ordering yet.' David's forehead was just a touch creased.

'We'll get food that'll go with the wine then,' said Merv, and began his earnest consultation with the wine waiter.

Amanda was talking. ' . . . They put in a new gearbox

last month but it's still not right. I was stuck for hours in the traffic, so boring. I thought of this slogan: 'Take a tube, it's not worth the traffic.' 'What do you think Ray?'

The atmosphere round the table relaxed, all the faces turned to Amanda, sickly little plants under the ministrations of a sun lamp.

Jackie undid the top button of her blouse.

'It is warm,' agreed Ray, catching her gesture. He had a piece of paper neatly folded and a pen poised. 'If everyone's ready?'

'You bet your life we are,' chorused Merv on his own.

A waiter stood fixed in an efficient curve at Ray's elbow. He waited while orders were countermanded, instructions were ignored, advice was taken, only to be rejected, and final decisions were reiterated again and again, only to be changed at the last moment. Small spots of red appeared on Ray's cheeks as for the third time he wrote in Duck Special. The waiter had yet to write anything at all. Amanda wasn't even paying attention, she was laughing at some inaudible but probably dirty joke that Merv was telling her.

When the waiter finally left a babble of conversation arose, irritable and high-spirited with hunger and a little too much drink. There were already three more bottles on the table. Jackie usually only drank one glass of wine with any meal but she was now sipping away at her second without a qualm. Around her raged a detailed dissection of a minor television personality with whom half of those at the table had worked. It was probably her imagination that everyone was suddenly talking if not more loudly, certainly more clearly. Aggie was looking impressed, she was smiling at Ray, who was pretending not to notice. Aggie didn't mind being here just as 'Ray's girlfriend'.

'Do you have to talk shop?' Gail inquired. 'You lot always do, and I can tell you right now —'

'Of course we don't,' said Amanda immediately, putting a restraining hand on both Ray and David. 'We must be terribly boring the way we go on.'

'Yes,' said Gail.

There was the slightest pause before Merv decided to entertain the table with an account of his and Sue's last visit to her parents. Every time he achieved some extreme in savagery and sarcasm Sue was compelled to cap it. '. . . By this stage the old bastard was totally and disgustingly pissed.' Merv blew his cheeks out in an imitation of florid rotundity. A slight spray of red wine sprinkled onto the table cloth. David, in his new expensive linen suit, kept stoically still. 'Shoot the bloody blacks and that'll stop the bloody riots.' Merv raised his glass. 'Shoot anyone suspected of a suntan.'

'He poured bleach in my bath as a child,' said Sue. Aggie looked astonished.

'I'm absolutely starving,' announced Amanda. 'I could eat a horse.' She paused. 'What a horrible expression.'

'People eat anything if they're hungry,' said Ray, who was aware that any moment his stomach would go into full orchestral action. At the moment it was rumbling darkly, quietly.

'Aboriginals,' said Sue carefully, 'aboriginals eat millipedes.' Aggie looked sick.

'Where?' challenged Merv, his eyelids at half-mast. It was a look he had borrowed off Charles Laughton he had told Jackie soon after David had introduced them. He was a film buff. They were all film buffs in fact.'Where?''I read it in a book.'

'Did people ever eat horses I wonder.' Amanda looked anxiously at Merv, then Sue, who both looked more than a little like horses themselves in that overbred English way. 'They're so beautiful,' she protested.

'They still do in France,' Jackie said. 'Eat horses I mean. It's not that common of course but you can get some in most meat markets if you look. It's not as popular as it once was. I think it wasn't economically viable. To breed horses for meat.'

'Christ,' said Gail, clicking her bright, blood-coloured nails against the ashtray. They looked like red beetles, carnivorous beetles thought Jackie, who above all wanted a distraction. She felt David would think she had just made a fool of herself. She looked up and caught sight of a procession of plate-bearing waiters wheeling into view. It took them one minute and thirty-four seconds precisely to lay out the dinner before their avid eyes.

'Thank you very much,' said David gravely.

The waiters bowed and withdrew in formation.

'Looks marvellous,' Amanda called out after them.

Of course they all used chopsticks, only Aggie appeared to have serious difficulties.

'More, more. More,' laughed Amanda as Merv and David both piled her plate with titbits. She looked so happy. It was understandable that she was happy — she was kind, intelligent, uncomplicated, generous and good-looking and nobody, even the most suspicious the most cynical, could fail in the end to love her.

'To Amanda,' said Ray, his eyes beaming, his glasses catching the light. 'To our lovely Amanda. Happy birthday.'

Everyone raised a glass and clinked them together. All round the table lapped an affectionate lull. Merv filled the wine glasses again.

'What's this prawn thing?' asked Gail, poking it with her chopsticks. 'It's not too fattening,' said Sue nastily. As Gail paused to reply, Amanda interjected, 'You shouldn't say that. Gail's been a hero about her diet.' 'It's OK. Sue's always like that when she's premenstrual,' said Gail, efficiently swallowing string after string of bean sprout. 'And how do you know she's premenstrual? You been sniffing around again?' asked Merv. Aggie looked shocked.

'There's no one to beat the Chinese at cooking,' said Ray, breaking into his first real sweat of the evening.

'Oh. Oh. Oh,' called out Aggie in a weak shrill voice. David instinctively drew his chair away from her, which was just as well as into her lap shot a large prawn coated in hot red sauce. 'I dropped it. I dropped it.' Aggie's London accent became, if possible, even more pronounced. 'I've burnt myself.'

'Let me look, I'm into first aid,' leered Merv, smiling across the table. Gail, who had just lit up, blew smoke out in his direction. 'Are you alright?' Jackie asked as Amanda got up and round the table and dabbed at Aggie's dress with a napkin, splashing the contents of the finger bowl all over the table.

One of the waiters in an attitude of impassive enquiry appeared at the entrance.

'It's perfectly alright,' David said to him. 'We're fine,' he went on crossly, his lower lip stuck out just short of a sulk. Whose fault was it that he wasn't enjoying himself? These were his closest friends, it didn't make sense that he was this bored in the company of his closest friends.

Aggie by this time was speechless, red faced, near to tears. Amanda poured her another glass of wine, and one for Ray because he looked so gloomy. Jackie drained her own glass in sympathy. 'We'll all have another drink,' said Merv. 'Jackie's the right idea. Cool, calm and collected, look at her. While the rest of us are flapping about like — here.' He lifted the offending prawn from Aggie's sideplate. 'Here Gail.' He dangled it in front of her nose. To his surprise she snapped it greedily from his fingers, one gulp and it was gone. 'I was a piranha in my previous existence,' she said. 'Or a killer whale,' Merv said. He poured himself a very full glass and made a point of passing the bottle over to Jackie. 'No,' said Gail. 'That's what I am now. All twelve stone of me.'

'You must think we are very adolescent,' whispered Ray to Jackie.

'Not at all,' said Jackie politely.

'Merv isn't as bad as he seems you know.' Ray pushed his glasses up his nose. 'I suppose we none of us are.' He barked a laugh. Jackie for one more countless time in her life could think of nothing to say. Luckily Ray was leaning forward, his face slightly moist with benevolence, saying,' . . . people really. When you get to know us. You see, it's all good humoured, at bottom. Even Gail and Merv once you know the situation. I expect David's explained the set-up.' She was aware that round the table light, bright balls of conversation were being juggled by these past masters of that elegant art. Even Aggie, half hysterical at some remark from someone, had found a niche and was clinging to it. Ray was still talking.

'A bit intimidating,' he confessed cosily. 'Intimidating to me, but then I'm easily intimidated. I'm not very good socially at the best of times and with very glamorous people I just go to pieces. I'm no good at small talk, you see, and I'm not good looking. Women like men who are good looking.' He was looking at her expectantly and she was resolutely smiling back. It would be easy to make him laugh, to reassure him, to say that looks did not matter or that, personally, she found nervous, bald men deeply attractive. It wouldn't matter, it would be meaningless.

'You two getting on famously I see,' said Sue exactly on cue. Her eyes were glittering with drink.

'I'm sorry,' said Jackie, more to herself than to either of them. Ray had turned away, clearly disappointed. He would dislike her now, he might even say something to David. Not that that should worry her, David appeared to take no notice of anything anyone said to him.

'Do you really think we need any more wine?' asked Ray in an unhappy voice as Merv called a waiter over yet again.

'Yes, I do,' said Jackie.

Merv smiled at her. 'Bravo, my love. Well bloody said.' He poured the last dregs from all the dead bottles into a glass and passed it over to her with a flourish. 'Can't have David's lady thirsty can we?' He leant his head back theatrically and laughed. The outline of his Adam's apple was painfully exposed.

The dormouse in *Alice in Wonderland* that's who I am, thought Jackie. That's a relief, I can just go to sleep in the teapot, or in this case under the table.

'Will you look at the state of the tablecloth,' invited Amanda. David was looking. 'Look at the mess we've made.'

'Pigs at a trough,' said Ray, who calculated he must have put on at least three pounds in the last hour.

'Some of us were,' said Gail smugly.

Ray would have liked to say something but couldn't. After all she was his boss.

'I'll have to go to the toilet,' said Aggie.

'Off you go then,' said Sue. She had spotted the waiter coming up, a brace of bottles in his hands.

'Shall I come with you?' offered Amanda.

Aggie, at last, stood up. The stain of the dropped prawn roundly and redly displayed across her lap.

'Well at least you're not pregnant, look at it that way,' said Merv, and they all laughed, even Ray, especially Ray.

'Does it really show?' she asked.

'No.' 'It's fine.' 'It's terrific, honestly.' 'You can't see a thing.' Nobody seemed to be able to stop giggling and when they saw Aggie's erratic progress across the restaurant and the reactions it produced in the other customers, the table collapsed in uproar.

The only one not laughing was Jackie. She was wondering if she'd always been a self-righteous bitch.

'Christ,' wept Gail. 'Stop it Merv for God's sake.'

'I don't think Jackie's very amused.' Sue looked all the way down from her six-foot to Jackie's five-foot-zero. 'Jackie's a very serious girl,' said Ray. 'Well I agree. I don't think we should have let Aggie go out like that. On her own,' said Amanda. 'Looking like . . .' she trailed off and she hit Merv with her napkin to keep from laughing.

'I'm sorry,' said Jackie.

'Oh stop bloody apologising,' said Gail, yawning. 'God laughing makes one feel so bloody post-coital.'

'I thought you were celibate,' said Ray, and blinked to show he meant nothing personal.

'I am,' said Gail. 'Oh yes I am.'

'Maybe you should go on one of those assertiveness training thingies,' suggested Sue to Jackie. At this stage of the evening it was touch and go with Sue. She could get either philanthropic or plain vicious. 'You could take Aggie with you.'

'Is somebody talking about me?' asked Aggie, appearing. She looked very pale. 'What's going on Ray?'

she said, her voice sharp, like a twig breaking.

The waiters appeared, and as practical as punctuation broke up the conversation by beginning to clear the table. The fallen rice they flicked neatly onto the floor, everything else they gathered up and bore off.

'Does anyone want a dessert?' Ray said looking bright and intelligent. Bereft temporarily of her ashtray, Gail was looking vulnerable. Catching her anxious look he added, 'Apart from Gail that is.' 'Christ Ray.' 'I didn't mean . . .' Two hot little spots appeared on his cheeks.

'You know what I think,' Sue began. 'Does anyone care darling,' said Merv, who had produced a long thin cigar from somewhere and was rolling it ostentatiously between his fingers. He was the kind of man who looked better asleep, Jackie decided, doing nothing.

'We'll all have coffee I think,' David said to the waiter.

Jackie watched him sitting there, his finger pressed lightly against the side of his nose, the faintest of protests against the draughts of cigarette smoke Gail was exhaling. He was calmly, and quite obviously, watching the antics of the others. In his role of judicious observer he managed to keep the lightest trace of control over the proceedings. Nothing could get too seriously out of hand with David there. In that knowledge certain self-restraints could be abandoned. Merv, as David's oldest friend, took the fullest advantage of this.

It wasn't David's reserve she envied, she was reserved herself, it was his lack of self-criticism. Rolling round in her head like the vanes of a windmill was the dull clatter of her thoughts, grinding nothing, neither wheat nor chaff. Nothing she could do to shut it up, shut it off, her self-consciousness. She finished off her glass of wine, her eyes had the faintest prickle of tears. 'It's great coffee,' she said with self-contempt. 'It's not usually that good in Chinese restaurants.'

'I think, my dear old darlings that it's time we all burst into a heartfelt rendition of that old favourite "Happy Birthday".' High as a kite, Merv swayed on his feet with only the thinnest of strings to anchor him.

Ray had sunk into a depression. Back and forwards he swished the wine round his glass. He was wondering why it was that women like Amanda, or even Amanda herself, never slept with him.

In the meantime David, charming David who had at last decided to charm, pushed Merv back into his chair and with a delicate dancing chopstick in his hand began to sing. Ray when pointed to joined in with his Paul Robeson voice and then Merv followed. Sue came in with a rush and then Gail more soberly. 'Lovely,' encouraged David, 'quietly now but all together.' One by one over the first few lines each voice slipped into harmony. Amanda, convulsed with laughter, looked both pretty and ridiculous, like an over-excited child. Everyone's face was shiny with heat, food, wine and now good humour. With his improved baton David led them in and out of chorus after chorus, keeping them in tune, keeping them together. All that is except Jackie, who sat silent, the heels of her hands pressed together and her eyes fixed down.

'Oh why didn't you sing,' said Aggie. 'It was great fun.'

'I've an awful voice.'

'Some people have,' agreed Amanda nodding.

'There's nothing wrong with her voice,' said David.

'I do have a lousy voice.'

'She's just being awkward,' David continued unperturbed. He always spoke slowly when he wished to wound.

Ray gave Jackie a malicious look and smiled.

'Never mind,' said Amanda brightly.

Jackie felt the rock lift off her back and now she was out and crawling in a bright and unknown world.

'David. . .' she said. He looked calmly at her. She had failed him, she had not come up to scratch. He was so physically perfect, it was hardly worth sleeping with him, she'd be better off with a photograph. 'There's no need to go on about it,' he advised, buffing the nail of his little finger with the clean corner of his napkin. All eyes were on him. Jackie wished with all her heart that he would stop. She wished he would throw that napkin down and say to her, let's go, let's leave. There is no need for you to feel self-conscious and sarcastic. It is not your fault, and either way you are forgiven. Let us go home and be simple and affectionate, as simple and affectionate as sea anemones. Assuming that they were simple and affectionate.

'Perhaps we could have another coffee,' suggested Amanda.

'It's really very good for a Chinese restaurant,' said Gail vaguely. 'The coffee.'

Jackie felt the undignified rush of tears fall down her face. She did not let a muscle on her face move or any sound escape her. Suddenly her hand was violently crushed.

'Don't,' said Sue fiercely out of the corner of her mouth. Then, letting go of Jackie's hand, she deftly lifted the last bottle and split what was left between their two glasses.

'I shouldn't drink any more,' whispered Jackie.

'Why not? Why the hell not?' asked Sue.

'It's not. . .' Jackie made a vague but she hoped understandable gesture. 'It's not that. I'm not upset about that.' It was peculiar the way her eyeballs felt as though they were being barbequed. She didn't know if it was because she was drunk or because she was crying. 'You see today, today is a very special day to me.' The company was trying to break up into intimate *tête-à-têtes* but Jackie plunged on regardless. She blew her nose on the napkin. 'It's my parents' anniversary,' she said to the faces turned reluctantly in her direction. She didn't look at David. 'Not their wedding. It's the anniversary of the day they died.' Her mouth was dry with panic but a smooth voice went on. 'It was a car accident.' Jackie listened to that quiet dreamy voice saying, 'They were driving up from Dover. They always went to Brittany around Easter, they were very fond of northern France.' Gail waved her packet of cigarettes in Jackie's general direction. 'I don't smoke. I gave up smoking.'

'Let her talk,' Amanda admonished. 'It's good to talk.'

'They didn't usually take the night sailing but that was all they could get. There were fog warnings but you know how people ignore them. They were on the road, it was very early, when round the corner came this enormous articulated lorry. It was going at over sixty.'

'I hate night driving,' said Merv.

'Dad was a good driver but what could he do. They were just driving slowly along because of the fog warnings when round the corner came this enormous articulated lorry. I've said that haven't I.'

'Never mind.'

Jackie blinked like a patient in a hypnotic trance. 'Do you know what was in that lorry?'

'No,' said Aggie. 'No,' said Amanda, her body pressed against the table as she leaned over to take Jackie's hand.

'Guess. Just guess.'

'Just tell us for Christ's sake,' snapped Merv.

'Chickens. Frozen chickens. They must have bounced like bullets all over the road.' The voice now was very light, airy.

'Perhaps you should take her home Davy boy,' Merv said in a stage whisper.

'I wasn't in the car,' she continued, because nothing was going to stop her now. 'It was the first time they'd gone without me. I was sixteen and they said I could stay with a friend. I was there when the phonecall came and Angela's mother woke me up.'

Aggie was falling asleep, her head on Merv's shoulder. He sat bolt upright.

'I had to go to the hospital. It took us hours to get there. Everyone was kind, they were very kind. There was only me you see. I was an only child. I still am.' She gave the faintest of smiles. 'There was only me to identify them. They took me into this room. It was the coldest room in the world.' Every detail was getting through to Jackie as she danced along on the high wire.

'It's OK,' Amanda whispered.

'Is it?' Jackie asked. 'Well then we walked over to the corner of the room and then someone suddenly just pulled this drawer out of the wall. A giant filing cabinet and there under a sheet —'

'Don't,' said Ray. 'Don't.'

'Dad wasn't too bad, because he'd been driving the damage must have been mostly to the chest, which I didn't see.' Gail nodded. Jackie had them all now firmly fixed on her. 'But poor Mummy, poor Mummy it was like . . . You know the way you tear open an envelope — say it's a love letter or something you've been waiting for, you just grab it off the mat and tear it open.'

'It's outrageous,' said Gail, clearing her throat, 'making a child of that age . . .'

'There was only me, you see,' said Jackie.

'They could have found somebody else,' agreed Sue. 'No.'

For the first time that evening Jackie relaxed back totally into her chair. She had taken all her boats out to sea and burnt them. If David had not guessed that she was lying, and lying for no reason, despicably, he would soon find out. And that would be that. She leant even further back into the chair, tilting it. A waiter appeared with the bill, he dropped it softly down between David and Amanda.

'I love you,' Jackie said loudly. She hadn't a care in the world.

Griz

This is Griz's story.

She was not unique, in fact she was number eleven. The previous ten had performed within that adequate average that is preferred, so there was little hesitation in authorising an eleventh. Certain modifications were added to the basic printout, some to improve performance and others no doubt the result of artistic inspiration. There is something about genetic holograms that tempt even the most experienced technician to try a realignment here, a tiny twist there. There can be no question however, of any gross interference. After a period of just less than eight months the new warp, Griz, was successfully decanted. At inspection she was declared perfectly adapted and released to the creche.

The first year of any creature's life, real or created, is a difficult and a delicate time. Immense care is taken in the warp creche to provide the exact environment that will ensure the kind of development required. All physical needs are attended to regularly and promptly by warp-creche workers who have an almost maternal solicitude for their charges. Low red lighting, the absence of any hard objects, and the continuous tinkle of music all help to give the new warp a sense of safety and security.

Naturally during this period there is no contact whatsoever between the warps and unadapted humans. As the use of language is strictly prohibited in the creche there is little danger of rumour mongering. Aimless speculation is, in any case, of no use to warps.

When Griz's motor functions, compliance *etcetera* were calibrated on her second birthday, she was pronounced a good average. That would have made her happy if she could have understood the concept and more so if she had known the consequences of failure. All new warps leave the creche at two, regardless of destination, though there are few wastages these days.

On that day, then, the excited two-year-old was taken by two of the creche workers. They went down the corridor, Griz grimacing and making unspecific sounds. Warps experience and express very directly at this stage. The creche workers were silent and gave little response to her.

At the end of the corridor was a smooth flat object going from floor to ceiling in one serene flow. The warp workers recognised it immediately, for Griz it was extraordinary, an incomprehensible object. For the first time she was confronted with the work of the unadapted. The experience was probably similar in kind to those undergone by mystics. This is, of course, intentional.

Griz crouched there alone, shivering, her lips retracting rhythmically over her teeth. A great deal of personality-profile material is gleaned from a warp's response to abandonment in the face of an unknown and terrifying object. Most warps after innumerable forays and feints will touch the surface of that door, but the timing and the type of approach made will often decide the future course of the warp's existence. Griz live up to expectation here as on so many other occasions and finally touched down with the barest tips of her knuckles after twenty minutes.

Up slid the door and there were columns of colour, smells like teasing needles, abrupt and angular shapes and everything smooth, smooth like the inside of a mouth, but hard. Thus the warp is given a delayed but essential equivalent experience to the birth trauma. This enhances their natural tendency to need security, approval, before other less relevant desires. Griz came over the edge of her world into the illuminated life of real people. Guards with visored faces lifted her rigid body onto a trolley and wheeled her away.

The room they took her to was in the examination centre. Inside were four people ready to begin the final assessment of Griz's potentialities. Griz could make no sense of what she saw, nothing could have prepared her for creatures whose faces were made of skin.

'Griz,' said one of them when she had been harnessed into the chair, 'your name is Griz.'

'Oh, quickly,' said another.

'What's wrong with it?' said the third.

'Griz,' said the first again, and leaned over, into her face, baring its teeth at her. No toilet training could withstand that.

'Christ.'

'Oh, Griz, Griz,' panted one of them.

The chair flattened and they started their examination.

Next morning they began her education. She sat in the school-room, wearing red shorts, listening to the high human voice of a person called teacher. The first lessons were to shout lines and lines of words again and again. Good warps were given lunch. There must be no scratching or leaving of place. There were cubes to be placed in tubes and colours to match with colours. Good warps ate tea. Then they must run and swing, run and swing, over the bars, between the bars. Good warps went to sleep at the time called night.

The first period of warp education is undifferentiated. All are taught the basic skills, component assembly, language to Level III, obedience. The last is the most critical in the development of these 'intelligent instruments' as they have been called. It is a delicate but not a difficult task. Willingness is quite literally bred into the bone. There may be occasions when it is worthwhile to reinforce or even extend primary traumas, after all it must be remembered that adult warps, while rarely reaching human stature, frequently weigh eighteen stone with a musculature to match.

'This is you,' said the teacher. A stiff hairy face flashed upon the screen. 'See,' said the teacher, 'low cranial development. There was a writer once who described life as nasty, short and brutish,' the teacher panted. 'But it is a good description of you, isn't it?' Anxious warp heads nodded. 'And for contrast we have this,' the teacher said softly as a different picture emerged. 'These are people. Do you see? Even you can see I suppose.'

There are creatures that occur naturally and there are those that are created. What is natural has spontaneity, joy and always, even in the lowest life form, the possibility of development, of change. The artificial are dull, genetically blunt, their use is only in their usefulness.

'There are those who might place you between the animals and us, the unadapted.' The teacher's head shook and the warps shook their heads as well. 'You are not. You are nowhere near. We are part of God's creation, you are the creatures of convenience.'

When Griz had graduated to yellow shorts, the teacher told her it was time to be assigned. Griz crouched, resting her weight on her knuckles. 'So Griz,' he said kindly, 'do you know what must happen now?' Griz began to make swift repetitive movements with her hands. 'I give you permission,' said the teacher. 'You may speak.'

Griz rocked a little, then spoke. 'I work.'

'And how will you work?'

'Work hard. Work hard.' She patted the floor for emphasis.

'You must work hard,' agreed the teacher. 'You must work hard and then you will be a good warp.'

Griz waited.

'You are strong. It is good to be strong. Your strength is your service. Tomorrow you leave here. Tomorrow you begin work. You will work in the steel mill,' said the teacher. 'This is your hat. You must be very happy.'

Griz put on the hat and was very happy. When she went to the steel mill, she did work hard, she was a good warp. Her strength and steadiness were commented on by the superiors. Their big voices boomed encouragement through the box. Day after day all the warps were encouraged. At night they could sleep.

Then one morning Griz woke up and she was puzzled. Her hair stiffened in a hot cloud around her body and there was this restlessness that wanted to scratch and bite. When the work-bell rang she screamed at it and threw herself up and down the sleeping shelves, frightening the other drowsy warps. Her teeth were bared, blood banged in her veins. Parts of her ached or felt angry. She wanted to guzzle her food. She wanted to waste it.

' Griz, ' she shouted. 'Griz.'

She shouted this although she knew the use of language was forbidden in the dormitories. Visored guards came and snatched her away.

Warps reach breeding maturity at around the age of eight. The hormonal onslaught experienced often results in irrational and sometimes even apparently violent behaviour. While there may be a degree of property damage during this period, there are rarely any attacks on personnel or on other warps. Due to the excellence of their education the instinct for self preservation is very seldom triggered even in the most threatening situation. There are innumerable experiments which back up this observation.

Warps themselves have a limited and very hazy concept of what used to be called reproduction. It is considered too abstract and theoretical a principle for a single-sex subspecies to grasp. There has been a wide ranging and stimulating debate on the intellectual ability of warps but all agree in the practical sphere it is better to underuse than to overstimulate.

It used to be the case that warps on reaching reproductive maturity were, with few exceptions, immediately neutered. The artificial wombs performed predictably, an important factor, and with an eighty-five per cent success rate. Since the development of bioflash technique, however, there has been a return to the traditional method of warp production. There are still some regrettable side-effects in using this technique on living adult bodies but the gestation period has been reduced from an eight-month to a five-month period. This is, of course, much more cost effective. There are many who advocate this method of warp replacement less on economic than aesthetic grounds. It is easy to see why.

In Griz's case it was decided to permit a pregnancy. A fertilised ovum was placed in the appropriate organ. Though not conscious during much of her pregnancy, it was felt that she underwent very little discomfort and almost no actual pain. The new warp, a Rak, number eighteen and an increasingly popular breed, was placed in the creche exactly on schedule. Griz was given a period of rest, not more than two months, before the second implantation. It is necessary to re-use breeding warps almost immediately as there are still problems with the bioflash program. Also the warps themselves do appear to find the process confusing or puzzling and it is advisable not to allow too much time to lapse between extraction and reimplantation. Three warps were successfully produced from Griz, an acceptable amount. But the fourth and fifth implantations were rejected. This is similar to the earlier problems of tissue rejection in organ transplants. These difficulties will be resolved in time.

The decision to return Griz to the steel mill may have been a bad one. She was not only older but also aged by the bioflash technique itself. It is also possible that the last pituitary gland correction may not have had the desired effect. Whatever the reasons, impairments were noted in reflective-reactive time, muscular elasticity and morale. All three factors could have contributed to the accident in which a major tendon was severed in her left leg. This lowered her productivity significantly. A reassessment was required.

The cell she sat in was dark and shabby. Smells were everywhere, smeared on the mattress, eddying round the ineffectual ventilating fan. The leg lay straight ahead of her, with the hair only beginning to grow back. Waiting was hard. She didn't like the dark or the smell her body was manufacturing. When they came and took her to the other room she bore her knuckles into the ground and held the pain in her leg silently. High, hard and quick the voices conversed over her.

'Griz,' said the final voice, 'we have a place for you. There is still work for you to do. Not too different from what you are used to. There is a truck this evening and it is going to the mines, to Alto, a very special mine. You will be on that truck.'

She was on that truck, strapped in a harness of smooth plastic. Each warp had a separate compartment, kept scrupulously clean by an ingenious system of sluicing. This was necessary as the journey to the uranium mine took ten days and it was important that warps arrived disease-free and clean. The compartments were not quite sound-proof. Griz could hear quite clearly the endless scratching of nails. There was even a voice making sounds on her right.

'Hello, hello, hello,' said the voice, a warp-voice. It was strange to hear a disembodied warp-voice. It was only the unadapted that spoke in places where they could not be seen. It was a skill they had, to speak from anywhere, from the past even, and always to be obeyed. ' Hello, hello, hello, ' the voice went on. Griz put her hand over her mouth, embarrassed.

Warps are not designed for skill in verbal communication. They can usually express direct intention, agreement or a desire for more instructions, but all in the most rudimentary fashion. It is true that they have developed some kind of sign language which they appear to use to convey emotional states or possibly trivial bits of information to one another. It can be an appealing sight watching a group of warps gesturing to one another, it can look quite attractive.

One by one they dropped from the back of the truck and down onto the dusty road. How curious they were, even for warps, singe-skinned or one-eyed, some with twisted limbs and one, strangest of all, whose bald face grotesquely mimicked the unadapted. Defects and rejects all, they crouched breathless in the thin air of mountain station Alto. They were panting, not just from the lack of oxygen but from the sudden appearance of the high flat lid of the sky, wider than all the world it seemed. Their hands gripped the ground, their muscles locked in agoraphobia. The truck drove away.

In the shadow of the mountain two or three warps hooted, their arms beckoning the newcomers. It was many minutes before those on the roadway could do more than whimper and scurry in the dust. The first one to escape from under the open sky was the bald-faced warp, and once in safety she shouted: 'Come on, come on.' Griz pretended it was the voice of an unadapted human and managed to work her way over to the tunnels.

The tunnel where the warp workers were housed were deep, that could be smelt, but sleeping shelves and the eating area were very near the entrance. Griz was given dry biscuits and dripping meat, she ate that and she drank the water. Younger warps were still panting, a sound similar to laughter but having little relation to comic relief. In the dark, hands groomed her and led her up to a sleeping shelf. She rested the ridge of her spine against the back of the mountain and slept.

In the morning the bell rang. They all raced in a bundle to the entrance of the tunnel.

'Come out. Come on then. Let's get going,' said the voices. Squinting and shuffling, the warps eased out, the newcomers staying well within running distance of the tunnel. Griz kept her hand on the rockface. In front of her stood a whole group of the unadapted. It was hard to see their white faces in the white light.

'Warps, look at me.' The warps old and new looked.
' I am the man in charge here. That's the man I am. These
other men are your bosses. This place is a mine. You dig
the ore here. That's what you do. You work hard, my
warps. That's what you do, you work hard.'

Griz had never seen so many of them, all together.
Their slight, delicate bodies stretched half a head taller
than any warp's. One of them bent down to a container at
his side and lifted out a strangely shaped and sharp
smelling object. The man threw the object in the dust in
the middle of the compound, threw another, another,
another. There was tension all around Griz.

'OK, OK' said the man in charge. 'You got your bets
placed gentlemen?' The gentlemen spoke quickly together. The man waited. 'Go,' he shouted.

There was a spectacular rush of hairy bodies. Some
were pitching head-over-heels in the excitement. The men
were shouting encouragement. Griz ran over with the
rest, raced back to the rockface. Then she must try to run
again and get another object, but it was too hard for her
with that leg.

'OK,' shouted the man in charge. 'That's it. That's
got you well warmed up, I bet eh?' He walked over to
them, he was less than three feet away. 'Can't see more
than four, any of you warps get more than four? None of
you new warps cheated, took two at a time? Well it looks
like Ra's won again. And when Ra wins, I win. That's
true.' He rubbed his hand on the forehead of the young
and chattering warp, Ra. She was rocking on her heels,
happy. The man bared his teeth to the other men. 'OK,
gentlemen those that owe me pay up. And you girls can
eat your bananas.'

Griz was taken with a group of other warps in the
first truck. She ate her one banana, swaying with the
bumps. Opposite her was the bald-faced warp, she was
watching Griz. Griz felt herself stiffen when this warp
spoke.

'Your name is?' And when there was no reply, the
warp persisted. 'What is your name?'

'Griz.'

The man who drove the truck was near the engine and could not hear.

'I am Dav,' said the warp, 'but sometimes they call me Baldy. See.' She pushed her face, her hairless face, forward. 'They call me Baldy. The skinfaces do.'

In the mine tunnels they knelt, pneumatics in hands, while the dust rolled up and up and their breath clogged. When it was food time, Griz could not hold the bowl in her hands, her arms were so jarred. She had to lick the contents of the bowl like an animal.

'Oh. Oh. Oh.' moaned Baldy beside her, lying on her back in the dust, wallowing. 'Sleep time. Time for sleep.' The bell rang for work.

Bit by bit, day by day, Griz became adapted to the mine. She would work at the rock face, clean ore, sleep, eat as directed. Apart from the bent leg, there was little about her that the overseers noticed. Only those particularly malformed, or perhaps a good performer in the banana races, attracted much attention.

In both categories Dav, or Baldy, was prominent. There is something repulsive, even disturbing, about a warp flaunting a furless face. For this reason she was unique. It had been decided to allow development to see what other characteristics would emerge from this individual. Little of use had appeared and it was decided to move her to Alto and to remove her gene code from the Index. Still, as a runner in the morning races she was becoming popular with the men.

Griz was puzzled by Dav. All day she was hooting, scratching, sighing and chanting. At night in the dormitory to shocked silence she would walk upright like an unadapted and speak till her breath ran out in one long squeaking rant. She would talk and talk, not sense, just words. It was difficult to know why.

'I am the warp in charge,' she'd yell. 'Yes, Yes. OK. That's me. We need more ore. We need that ore. Work. Work well. Work hard my little warps. Bananas. Bananas,' she'd whine. 'Oh yes, bananas.' The performance would go on and on. Griz would put her hand on Dav's arm, try to groom her; but Dav would only hop from foot to foot, yelling louder and louder; 'I am the warp in charge.'

Obviously in some dim way, Dav believed that her furless face brought her closer to the level of humankind than the rest of the warps; though it must be admitted all warps are highly imitative. Certainly she did strive to run faster and faster in the banana race to attract the favourable notice of her overseers. One day she even beat the champion, Ra. A lot of the men banged their hands together to show their delight, though the chief man said nothing as he paid the one who had backed her.

'Good Baldy, good old Baldy,' said the man. 'That's the way. That's the spirit.' He lifted one of her arms high over her head. 'Isn't she a beauty.'

Dav had got five bananas that morning, she gave one to Griz in the truck on the way to work. She patted Griz's leg that was daily growing more stiff and useless. It was hard to endure the long hours crouched in the seams of the mountain with the machine writhing maniacally in exhausted arms. This was one time when a newcomer fell asleep at the rockface and the drill went sliding through the body of the warp next to her. Neither one was seen again after the shift was finished. Griz could be grateful that her leg was a goad to consciousness.

One night they were sitting, Dav and Griz, watching other warps gesture in the half-dark of the dormitory. The rock was cool and hard against Griz's back, cool and hard and a little damp. She was half-asleep, dreaming of dust, with Dav's voice buzzing like blue flies in her ear.

'Look, look.' Dav was pulling at her arm, impatient. ' Oh, Griz, ' she sighed, 'I win. Every day I win. You see Ra? Look at Ra. Look at Ra. Griz, look.'

What was Griz to look at? She was waiting for the sleeping bell. It was true that Ra had not won a race for weeks and the man in charge no longer spoke to her. It was true that her arms and legs were thinner and that all her weight had gone up into her swollen belly. Griz did not like to look at that belly.

'A little warp, a new little warp.' Dav swayed, mimicking the hoots called laughter. 'Yes. Yes. With the man in charge. OK. OK. What do you say, Griz? What do you say?'

Griz said nothing. This was not the first time Dav had mocked the way the unadapted produced themselves. At first Griz did not understand, but then she had heard the men talking. That was why they would take the truck down the mountains to the village some nights, singing. Warps could not sing either.

Next morning Griz saw Ra pour water on her biscuit. She saw her fingers dabble in the liquid mess and her tongue lick away at the mixture tiredly. Here was a place where teeth ached, hair fell out and hunger disappeared. It was the mine sickness. Ra's eyes blinked slowly. Sometimes dead or sick warps would have to be lifted onto the trolley and left until the men found time to clear them away. Griz went out of the tunnel into the bright day, where Dav danced with four bananas in her hand. The man who had picked her whistled when he saw Dav give a banana to Griz.

'Well,' he said. 'Well, would you believe that?' He shook his head and laughed. 'Come on girls, time for work. Come on champ,' he said to Baldy.

'OK, Sam,' Dav said to him. The man did not hear. Warps do not call the unadapted by their names. They do not speak at all unless commanded to.

The long day went on, with the conveyor belts slowly snaking their way up the surface. Griz did not wonder why these dull-coloured lumps were so prized by the man in charge. Work was work and must be done. She lowered the drill, coughed, raised the drill again. Coughing was something all warps did after a little while. She wished the water-bell would ring. All of them could hear that ring despite the noise of the drills. When they drank they could listen to the encouraging voices of the men that came even this far down, right to the bottom of the world. Out of the corner of her eye she saw Dav stagger with a

hod of waste on her back. When a warp with ragged ears
went to help, Dav bared her teeth and the other warp went
away.

'Come on, come on,' said Dav as she lay in the truck
that night. 'I'm hungry. Oh, I'm thirsty. Tired, tired
warps. Are you hungry warps?' Her head moved agitat-
edly from side to side. They lay like stone, stone-coloured
with crusted fur, on the floor of the truck, bouncing down
the mountain and back to Alto. There was the strained
sound of many lungs panting for oxygen although they
were outside and the air was everywhere for free.

There was always plenty of food, though some were
too tired or too sick to eat. Ra, for instance, stared from far
away at the feeding table, her big round belly cradled in
her arms. It seemed to Griz that Dav had never talked
more than she did that night, counting to numbers that
none had heard of, shouting orders, and saying things in
which there was no sense. Griz lay curled on her sleeping
shelf and did nothing. The sleeping bell rang.

It was in the middle of sleeptime, when good warps
are allowed to rest, that Griz was woken by a tugging on
her arm. Dav was looking down at her, her hand over her
mouth. Then Dav began climbing down the sleeping
shelves onto the floor and out towards the tunnel entrance. Without knowing why Griz followed her, but then
warps as previously noted are prone to imitative behaviour.

Dav walked carefully along the trackway that led past
the men's quarters. Overhead the moon drew the colour
out of everything. Minutes went by and still Griz followed, the breeze lifting the hair from her body. She did
not know if she was afraid. Never before had she been in
the open air so long, so unsupervised. They went past the
silent machines, the ragged rundown vegetation, and
began to climb up the rockface. There were voices ahead
of them.

Carefully they climbed, Griz holding her leg so that
not even the smallest of small stones was dislodged by a
clumsy movement. Up on the first ridge Dav waited for

Griz. They crouched together behind a boulder and looked down. They didn't speak, their hands were still.

Below them a pool of clear water lay. Streams from the high mountains fed it every spring with molten snow from the high passes. On hot nights, and this was a hot night, men would come here to swim, to cool down, relax. The warps watched submerged bodies breaking out of the water and diving down, utterly light and carefree. They were calling and clapping, talking in their fast musical voices and Griz, seeing them, felt the hair of her neck stiffen, and not with fear, not with strangeness, but with something that was not in the list of names she knew. Their bodies were pale and naked and they seemed to glow, like beings lined in light. Griz bowed her head.

'OK. OK,' whispered Dav. Griz turned to face her. It is unusual for warps to look at the eyes of another warp. Dav was still crouched, knuckles resting on the ground, but as she straightened Griz saw the rock in her hand. She saw the rock and the hand move through the air and the rock's release. She saw its disconnected flight down to the bathing men and its crash in the water. She saw the men's heads turning and twisting as they scanned the ridges around them. She heard instructions shouted. She saw body after body cover itself with cloth. She saw guns being grabbed. But none of this was as real as the grinding of Dav's fingers into her arm.

'Call out,' she whispered to Griz. 'Call. Call. Here we are.' She took another rock in her hand. 'This is the rock Griz. This is the rock in charge.' She tossed it between her hands, back and forth, back and forth.

Griz stiffened her body against the boulder and could not move. There was nothing to be done, she could do nothing. Dav bent her head to one side listening.

'For Christ's sake —'

'Just get moving, get up to the top and we can see what's what.''

'One lousy rock —'

'Yeah, one lousy rock.'

'I mean, Christ, what's the problem. I mean who's

going to come up here —'

'Stop complaining will you.'

The complaining man was Sam. Griz recognised his shoes. If the men turned their heads the warps would be seen. If they were seen Griz could not imagine what would happen them. Warps have a poor grasp of the future.

'It's kids I'm telling you. Just kids from the village, ' said Sam as they scrambled down towards the station. Griz could see other men following. They were alone on the mountain. Griz wished she was safe on a sleeping shelf, away. She would not listen to the words that Dav was saying. Hours passed, all was quiet and Griz began her stiff-legged scramble down the mountain. She could hear Dav moving carelessly behind her.

At the entrance to their tunnel, on a trolley, lay Ra. She lay with her belly humped over the thin tangle of her limbs. Dav softly scratched the highest point of Ra's stomach. Then she dropped her hand and hooted like a human laughing.

'No little warps,' she said. 'No little warps, eh Griz.'

Ra's eyes were still watery enough to glisten in a trick of moonlight. Griz could have closed those eyes. She looked at hands that could have closed those eyes, they were empty. She thought of rocks and wanted, absurdly, to rest her head against that distended belly.

The next day when Griz woke she was afraid. She would not sit with Dav in the feeding area, nor in the truck; quickly, without comment, she ate the banana Dav gave her. In a seam no bigger than her body she worked like a good warp, steady as a rock. Her hands gripped the drill, she gripped it like a creature drowning.

Dav herself was quieter in the days that followed, at the food or water-time she would sit twisting her head round, shaking it, batting it back and forward between her hands, whimpering. Soon the weather got cold, but it was always warm in the mines. Griz did not mind how hard she worked, how hot she got. At night she would wake with dreams of Dav cut open and huge rocks spilling out of her.

'OK, warps. Let's have a good race. Let's make this one count,' the man in charge called out. He was banging his arms against his body trying to keep warm. For the first time Griz looked at the clothes they wore and wished she could wear them, just for a while, just in the mornings. Dav was dancing, red-eyed with impatience.

'Your girl's impatient,' somebody called over to Sam.

Almost before the first fruit hit the ground, Dav was running. She was back at the rockface, clutching a banana and screaming with what seemed to be delight. Off she flew again, shoving a younger warp out of her way to get her next prize. Then, again, scattering the other warps with the furious speed of her running. In no time at all it seemed there was a pile of six or seven bananas. Griz could see the excitement the men were showing and the frantic exchange of words and money. The man with the stop-watch was counting down. Sam was yelling, banging the butt of his gun down again and again. They didn't seem to notice as one by one all the other warps dropped out of the running. They eddied up to the rockface, stayed there, some making confused, distressed gestures with their hands. Dav was running too fast for her face to have any expression.

'That's ten. Jesus, that's ten. It's a record,' shouted Sam. 'Come on baby. Come on.'

But this time she did not stop when she came to the line of bananas. In a maddened dash she came on. She punched her way through a group of men and really ran, really raced up to the cliff face that inclined straight up to the sky. Frantically she scraped a way up that surface while warps and men alike stared after her.

'Stop,' said the man in charge, but she couldn't. ' Stop, ' he said, but she didn't until the sudden sharp crack of the guns pumped bullet after bullet deep into her back and she dropped like a soft stone back onto the roadway.

The men Dav had levelled rose slowly to their feet in the silence, banging dust from their clothes. There was no talk, no gestures. All the faces were stiff and the men's guns were pointing directly at the warps for the very first time.

'Into the trucks,' said the man in charge. 'It's OK,' he shouted over to the men appearing from the huts ready armed. 'Just a mad old bitch run amok. Into the trucks you warps. Now.'

All day Griz did not know what to think, how to think. Warp 1Q rarely passes the lower fifties and Griz was only average. Warps anyway do not weep. On the sleeping shelf that night Griz rocked and swayed, crooning under her breath. She could not precisely formulate thoughts, but images went through her mind. She saw again the first door, the lights, the teachers and their shifting screens, her own blown belly, the fire, the furnace and finally the rockface. She remembered her life in the only way she could. Then clumsily she crawled out of the dormitory to find Dav's body, not realising it had been long removed.

There was a man at the entrance. He was sitting on the ground, nursing a gun.

'Well, who have we here,' said Sam. ''Who is this then?'

'Griz.'

'You come to keep me company eh?' he patted his gun. 'Felt sorry for me sitting out here all alone with my ass freezing to death?' He took a bottle from inside his jacket and tipped a long swallow down his throat. ''Did you know that dumb bloody warp? Baldy? Did you know her?'

'Yes,' said Griz.

'Doesn't make sense. I mean, the stupid warp gets a brain tumour, goes a bit crazy and bang she's dead. That's all there is to it. But old man Reynolds, he's the boss, he says we got to take precautions with you girls. We got to keep an eye on you. See nobody else steps out of line. So I'm sitting out here, getting frost-bite, to watch over a bunch of broken-down warps. Is that crazy?''

'OK,' said Griz.

Sam peered into the darkness, took another swallow of his drink. ''What you doing out here. You're supposed to be in beddy-bye aren't you?'

Griz coughed. 'Air,' she said.

'Lungs gone already are they? How long you been up here?' Griz shook her head. 'Don't keep track of time like we do I suppose. What'd you do before they shipped you out to Alto?'

'Work,' said Griz.

'It's pathetic, I swear to God it's pathetic.' Tears filled his eyes. 'Got nobody here to talk to except some stupid ugly bitch of a warp.' He laughed. 'They really don't take too much trouble over how you girls look, do they. I mean they could I suppose. Make working in Alto more fun if they did. Not many of the village girls are crazy about sleeping with us case they get sick. That's not how it works I told her. My genes may be a bit scrambled working up here but everything else's alright. It's more than alright.' He drank again. 'Those nice old genes my mammy and my daddy just whipped like cream. Just dust and ashes. How do you like that?'

'OK,' said Griz.

'Is that all you can say? Christ you really are dumb. Tell you one thing, when I get down off this mountain, I'm going to walk off here a real rich man. That's supposing I do walk off and they don't carry me feet first.'

'OK,' said Griz.

'Will you shut up?' he said, and swiped at her with the butt of his gun. He looked into her face, his eyes wavering. Griz said nothing. She watched him drink, she watched him talk. More than Dav ever did he talked, while his movements became blurred and frantic. He clutched at her shouting, twice he hit her, and as he slid half-asleep in the dust she kept looking at him. She felt her hands clench and found that in her right hand was a rock. She looked at the rock and the sleeping man. She looked at the rock and the man's head, beginning to see the connection.

Mr Haddington's Retirement

Peterborough, he thought, as he drove out of that city for the last time, is a bloody awful dump. Notable only for its beet factories with their sickly and unsubtle smell of burning sugar and well-sweated socks. In thirty-four years he had not grown used to it and now he need never smell it again. Those years could roll off his back, an undifferentiated lump of dead time, and sink with inertia out of his recollection. That was his plan. That was his route of escape.

At sixty-six, Mr Haddington looked exactly his age, neither more nor less. Being tall, thin and overshaved, he was the image of a particular type of retired schoolmaster, a man whose features would only become more whetted and sharpened with age. His voice had that hectoring tone of one long accustomed to addressing his intellectual inferiors, be they pupils or staff. In the dull, slightly lumpish atmosphere of St Edmund's school for young gentlemen he had preserved his dignity, his sanity, by a fixed and absolute solitariness. He had remained aloof from the clubbish bonhomie of the senior staffroom. There were few things more distasteful to him than the whimsicality of old codgers. He would not condescend to play a sub-Dickensian minor character for anyone's amusement. Generations of boys were indebted to him for his clear if chilly exposition of the mysteries of science. And if it was sometimes wondered what such a clearly talented, even brilliant, man was doing in the backwaters of a second-rate public school, no one had ever found the occasion to ask him. A lurid or criminal past or various of the more unusual sexual vices were humorously speculated on by younger staff members and by the pupils.

All that, all that weariness, all that stale recycling of similar years was behind him. Now was the time to allow for the slow unravelling of his accumulated experience. There was much to be done. There were fields of study to explore. There were monographs to write, essays, articles. He need have no regard now if these efforts were crowned with success or with failure. The indulgence of his intellect was at hand and only the Post Office in Peterborough had a forwarding address.

Fenwick was one of those small villages nearly deserted in the 'fifties then snatched from the brink and given the kiss of life by London stockbrokers. Aside from a small estate of neo-Georgian rustic cottages tucked down Dryers Lane, the place was hauntingly unchanged from his childhood. Not that he was a man to be haunted, and it seemed looking round the village that none of the aboriginal residents remained here or remained alive. Mr Haddington recognised not a name, not a face. He was a stranger here now and that was how he intended to stay, his social contact confined to the village shopkeeper and his over-freckled son. He was not here on holiday.

'Splendid,' he said to himself one morning as he stood in sodden slippers in the garden. 'Time for breakfast I think,' he said encouragingly.

He walked as briskly as he could with wet slippers

back into the kitchen, then straight into the study where last night's fire lay in a fit of exhaustion. Carefully he balanced the slippers at the correct angle to receive the maximum amount of available warmth. Then he looked down at the study table, its reference books, its ashtrays, its square sheets of paper covered with wizened little scribblings. He snatched up the top piece of paper and shook it as though trying to dislodge the creeping crawling words.

'What's this? What's this? Excuses, prevarications. Literature. Bloody literature. You're a scientist, speak up man, speak out.' He threw it on the fire. It took seconds to develop a singed appearance and even longer to burst into flame. 'Polly put the kettle on.' He went into the kitchen and did just that.

After breakfast he went up to the bathroom with all of last Sunday's papers. He had very particular views of the danger of rushing bowel movements and had no intention of sitting there with nothing but rows of winsome pouting goldfish to look at. He deplored the mind who could have conceived such wallpaper. Opening the paper exact centre he read inch after column inch detailing catalogues of conflict, catastrophe and corruption. There was nothing surprising in that, or in the fact that his hands turned an unlovely shade of charcoal so quickly. Both were equally inevitable. It was then the doorbell rang. It wasn't anyone he expected, there was nobody to expect.

An elderly man with a nodding smiling head said, ' Peter? ' his forehead wrinkling and unwrinkling uncertainly. Round his neck the large lasso of a clerical collar gleamed. 'Peter Haddington?' He glanced down at Mr Haddington's. unbuckled belt. 'Just up?' he asked hopefully.

'Excuse me —' began Mr Haddington.

'Don't apologise.'

'I wasn't.'

'Ah,' said the vicar with the air of a man accustomed to practicing patience.

'I am an extremely busy man. I am not a Churchgoer.
I require nothing from your organisation or its subsid-
iaries. I require only to be left in peace.'

'Peter Haddington?' repeated the vicar.

'Senile,' said Mr Haddington aloud.

The vicar blinked, his expression that of a sad old
tortoise coming round after a long unhappy hibernation.
'Joseph Ramsey. Vicar of St Mary's. Was. Retired now, of
course. Old friends you and I, and David of course, my
brother. Dead.' He took a gulp of air while Mr Haddington stared at the transformation of Joseph Ramsey.
'Very snug. Very snug,' said the vicar, peering round the
corner of Mr Haddington. Then with practised ease he
insinuated himself past and into the dining-room. It was
also the living-room and the study. 'Very comfortable.'
He gave the word a French accent. 'You've been here a
month haven't you? A month,' his head shook deprec-
atingly, or so it seemed.

'I'm a busy man,' said Mr Haddington.

The vicar's nodding head cast doubts on this and his
lips pursed in a meaningful way. 'I remember your father
of course. A good man. Not many of the old families left.'

'We were not one of the old families, if you remember, padre.'

'Must be nice, to return after sojourning in the vale of
tears. Quite the return of the native eh? Not the prodigal
son at all events. St Edwards wasn't it?'

'Edmunds.'

The Reverend Ramsey's head was all the while
swivelling round the room, missing not a detail. He saw
the papers on the table. 'Writing?' he suggested, and
began hovering round the room picking up and examining various discarded cups. There was little of the rugby
player left in him now thought Mr Haddington without
pity.

'When you have finished your inspection perhaps
you will find your own way out,' Mr Haddington framed
himself in the doorway. 'I've work to do in the garden.'

Sitting on the upturned wheelbarrow he wondered if,

after all, it had been a mistake to come back here. It was already difficult to decide if his return was planned as an act of defiance, or simply because he had no reason to be elsewhere. The cottage had been a bargain, it was comfortáble, comfortable, he sneered. There was a certain pleasure in seeing the decrepitude of the erstwhile stalwart Joseph Ramsey. He straightened his shoulders at the recollection.

'Fenwick,' he said firmly, daring the name to be evocative. There was happily nothing to sentimentalise in his childhood. No harvest homes, no sunset rides in the hay cart. Every evening, every morning, winter or summer he'd be out with the sons of the farm labourers picking stones from the fields and pitching them at the ravenous crows. He'd worked with the other boys and never made a murmur or a complaint though his father was the schoolmaster. While Joseph, David and Timmy Ramsey were safe asleep above their father's surgery he was out shying stones in Farmer Geddis's fields.

His father loved birds. Crows, magpies, anything that flew had a place in his affection, but favourite of all were the water birds. He'd travel miles every weekend to the fen country and there with his long black rubber boots and his broken binoculars chase after warblers and marsh birds, the migrators rare or ordinary. If Peter was with him he'd watch for the serious billed birds, the ones with legs like coathangers, walking stiffly and solemnly up and down the foreshore. His father would let him borrow the glasses for a precious few minutes but it was understood who had priority in their use. Peter would always hand them back before they were gestured for.

Yet this naturalist, this passionate ornithologist, let his son, his boy, earn half a crown a week by stone shying at crows.

Why? Why?

'The drunken bitch,' he said, and stamped his frozen feet. He walked away from his thoughts and back into the house.

Asleep on the sofa was the Rev. Ramsey, his head

scuffling against the grey moquette.

'Ripe. Cherry ripe,' said Mr Haddington, looking down at him. 'Almost over bloody ripe I'd say.' He made a move as if to shake him but shouted instead: 'Wake up. This isn't a sanatorium you know.'

One of the vicar's eyes opened immediate, the other seemed to be experiencing a difficulty. 'Chilly in here isn't it? Fire needs more coal I daresay.'

'I think better in the cold.' Mr Haddington sat on his working chair. He wanted to know for certain if the vicar had been looking through his papers.

'Like father, like son,' chuckled the vicar.

'My father,' enunciated Mr Haddington, 'my father hated the cold. He suffered from it all his life, chilblains, rheumatism, TB.' He stopped abruptly but the vicar was on another tack anyway.

'Lovely little articles he used to write for the *Gazette*. A real eye. Detail. Detail.' His head nodded emphatically. ' A rural schoolteacher but a truly gifted amateur naturalist. My father always had the highest, the very highest, regard —'

'Amateur,' said Mr Haddington angrily, his gaze fixed to the soft wrinkled face that grinned at him from the sofa, more naked, more ugly than any skull. Death is not a matter of bare bones, he thought, it would be better if it was.

'No offence,' said the old man, trying to lift up the poker.

'Give me that,' said Mr Haddington, and snatching the poker impatiently he began to beat the fire about. Smoke and ash filled the room.

The vicar immediately started coughing into a strangely small handkerchief, his wife's perhaps. 'Is there such a thing as water? A glass of water?'

'In the tap in the kitchen.'

'No matter,' sighed Rev. Ramsey.

'I presume you've been nosing your way through my private papers when I was in the garden,' Mr Haddington's face was set for coldness and fierceness.

'Indeed —'

'I find it extraordinary, it is extraordinary that any one even of your cloth, could presume on an acquaintanceship extinct for nearly fifty years, force the way into another man's house and while there rifle through his papers.'

'Peter,' said the vicar reprovingly, his head swaying sadly from side to side, 'you were always so prickly.'

'You must be nearly seventy.'

'Alas,' agreed the vicar. 'Two heart attacks to my credit. Minor of course.'

'It would be difficult to explain in layman's terms the exact nature of my field of study.' Mr Haddington made a steeple of his fingers, a habit he had when setting particularly tricky questions to an already bewildered class.

'Not at all,' said the vicar politely, trying in the meantime to detach himself from the oversoft sofa.

'This is a work,' said Mr Haddington, 'not of speculation, however recondite, but the product of a process of deductive reasoning.' His throat cleared but he had enough restraint not to read aloud, he merely looked the picture of absorption bending down over the papers.

The vicar in the meantime had managed to roll himself onto his feet and slyly sneaked out of the study. Mr Haddington waited, with a curious sensation in his chest, for the front door to click behind his first, his unwanted visitor.

'I took the liberty,' said the vicar, exhibiting a glass of water in his hand. He looked round the room hoping to sight some place other than the sofa to sit on.

'It is my view that the rot started with relativity,' announced Mr Haddington.

Meekly the vicar sat on the sofa. Now it was a question of getting his mouth to the glass or the glass to his mouth, whichever. 'Everytime I have a drink I get hiccups. Cup of tea. Hiccups. Water. Hiccups. Lord knows what people must think.' He gave a wheeze like an old concertina collapsing from leather fatigue.

'Where did you find that glass?' All the glasses

should be in the sideboard to his right.

'There was something in it,' admitted the vicar.

'A specimen. That isn't a drinking glass.' A slight malicious smile turned the corners of his mouth down.

'Since Mary died I seem to have lost interest in my hobbies,' said the vicar, his head nodding in sad agreement. 'I was a stamp man.'

Mr Haddington remembered how the Ramsey brothers' uncle had showered them with exotically stamped postcards from all over Latin America one hot envious summer in his youth. He wrinkled his nose.

'Never married. You never married. Best thing probably. It's worse for you then when they go before.' His blue eyes were washed with colour. 'People are very kind.'

Abruptly Mr Haddington got up and poured half a bucket of coal onto the fire.

'Very kind, given an opportunity,' amended Rev. Ramsey. 'Given the opportunity.' He was about to say more when he noticed a packet of firelighters hidden under a copy of the *Radio Times*.

'I do not find people kind. I find nothing about them kind. Brutal egotistical animals afflicted with the herding instinct.'

The vicar had managed to hook the packet onto his lap. He was trying to sneak a block out without disturbing the flow of Mr Haddington's thoughts. The cellophane was difficult to open and, loathing the taste of paraffin, he was reluctant to tear it with his teeth.

'To tinge science with the miasma of mysticism,' intoned Mr Haddington. 'That is the unforgivable sin, if one must believe in sin.'

'We must all respect each other's beliefs,' agreed the vicar, the cellophane wrapper resolutely refusing to rupture.

'It is nothing to do with belief.' The old fool is senile. He always was senile, from a boy.

'We all stand in need of the Grace of our Lord,' said the vicar with conscious simplicity.

'It doesn't surprise me that you would take refuge in the consoling clichés of your Church. But the question is —'

The Reverend had finally extracted a small piece of firelighter, the thing to do now would be to insert it as deeply as he could into the heart of the non-existent fire. He knelt on the rug.

'Get up man,' said Mr Haddington. 'Dear God, James, there's a time and a place for everything. I'll have no pious posturings in this house.'

'Have you a match?'

Mr Haddington passed him a cigarette lighter. Rev. Ramsey remained crouched there while the paraffin flared and dust rose up the chimney.

'I feel the cold,' confessed the vicar. 'Tell me this, you should know, does the blood actually get thinner as one gets older. It's not as red, I know.'

He was surprised when Mr Haddington helped him up and even more when he lowered him back down onto the sofa. They looked at one another for a moment in silence. They felt the presence of two young uneasy ghosts longing to escape this room, these occupants.

Mr Haddington lowered his head. 'The fault has always been in viewing ourselves as the apex, the resolution of evolution. What proof have we that we are the last product of creation.'

'We most certainly are not.'

'Oh yes,' said Mr Haddington. 'Well let's steer clear of what you mean by that. Let's keep religion out of it. '

'I am a vicar,' reminded the Rev. Ramsey, his head trembling.

'I don't care if you're the bloody Pope,' snapped Mr Haddington. 'Christ, man, will you listen. What I have here,' he gave his papers a thump of affection, 'clearly, precisely laid out —'

'You always were a prickly person,' said the vicar the nods of his head now slow and significant.

'I can see why they retired you. Incapable of a rational conversation.' He walked over to the sideboard, impatiently unlocked both the drinks cabinet and the glasses cupboard. He poured one glass of dark-brown sherry and, hesitating, recklessly poured a second. This he handed over to the vicar.

'Thank you Peter.'

Perhaps it was the tone of voice, its patrician courtesy that caused Mr Haddington to hiss: 'You and your bloody family.'

'At least my mother —' said the vicar, and shut his voice off.

'Ah,' said Mr Haddington, reseated, his long legs extending as the vicar shrank back upon the cushions. ' Ah.'

'Look I'm very sorry,' said the vicar. 'Very sorry. Bad tempered old goats, the pair of us. Specially me.' He paused. 'Mary used to keep a couple down the paddock. Haven't bothered since.'

Mr Haddington supped his sherry, his eyes half-closed, giving nothing away. He knew well enough that at moments like this, one's opponent was likely to make the most interesting, the most fatal exposures.

'It is difficult to lay down one's burdens, even if one is weary, even onto young, strong shoulders,' the vicar spoke authoritatively. For some reason when drinking alcohol his hand steadied. 'I was vicar here for most of my working life, you know. Most of my working life. I know how it feels, one looks back over one's life, over one's successes, one's failures, and one feels this nagging sense, of not exactly disappointment but . . . How long were you at St Edwards?'

'Edmunds.'

'How long were you at St. Edmunds?'

'Thirty-four years.'

'Your father would have been proud of you.'

'Don't raise your hand to me,' warned Mr Haddington.

'My hand?' said the vicar, looking at his half-raised right hand with surprise.

'I think you were about to bless me.' Mr Haddington

poured himself another schooner of sherry but the vicar demurred. 'What killed David?'

'The second world war,' said the vicar promptly, and Timmy went with a heart attack. The last survivor, that's me. And you now of course. From the old days.'

'Sentimental old bugger,' said Mr Haddington with a not pleasant smile.

'The village has changed of course, but not as much, not as much as it might have.'

Mr Haddington had no time to waste in replying to this remark, he had an urgent need to return to the subject of his own ideas. 'My father taught me one very major thing. Observation, he always said, that is the first task of any true scientist. Don't begin with a theory, don't be tempted to summarise, and be wary of conclusions.'

'An admirable man.'

'An amateur, I'll admit that, a man who for various reasons could not achieve those things he was clearly capable of.' A piece of coal cracked audibly in the grate, the vicar started. Mr Haddington smiled. 'Your wife — '

'I don't think she needs to be brought into the conversation.'

'A good wife no doubt, limb of your limb. Devoted, sober.' The word sober inspired Mr Haddington to pour another drink. Despite protests he filled the vicar's glass as well, splashing some on the vicar's old greenish trousers. 'I picture her, hard-working, gossiping, genteel, a little bit superior. Mary, Mary, quite, quite contented with her lot in life. What was the point of all that eh? All that getting up, all that drinking and eating, shitting and sleeping. Why in the name of God? What was the point of it? For her I mean, for anyone else come to that. What priceless, peerless contribution did she make to anything? Why should she be expected to anyway?'

He went on talking, an inexhaustible train rushing into an endless tunnel. Down in the darkness could be heard troubled hootings and the rattle of iron wheels locked into position. The Rev. Ramsey drifted into sleep with the same ease as he drifted back into wakefulness.

'Omnivorous. Do you understand what that means. I'm not talking about food. Man does not live by bread alone. Ha! We get from anything we can, cabbage or crocodile, pig or pineapple, we'll digest the lot. And rightly, rightly.'

He's getting over-excited, thought the vicar placidly. It was a curious fact that his attention withdrew at the least sign of shouting. This had given him a reputation for calmness and imperturbability, assets necessary for a minister who must, by the nature of his calling, deal with other people's crises. And the fire was in full fury now, he could feel the heat licking his legs. It was easy to slip gracefully back to sleep.

'Both in our own ways, willing enough to accept our place in the universe, I grant you that. The material world bathed in a rational light, or in your case peered at through a glass darkly, but I'll admit the similarities. There was structure, there was sense, there was, most important of all, the logical progression. Slowly, too slowly perhaps, we moved forward. I don't want to hear how history repeats itself or doesn't. I don't want to read their filthy novels. The man who wrote the *Tao of Physics* should be burned at the stake. You'd understand that, wouldn't you, that's one thing about the Christian tradition — it's serious, it was serious. Gone to seed now like everything else, to rack and ruin.'

The vicar felt he might never move again, enervated by the heat, the drink, the extreme softness of the sofa and the meandering voice of this silly fellow still living in an urgent adolescent fever. It was probably all fake. He must have taken the measure of himself by now. Of course, many schoolteachers do become curious cases of arrested development, stunted. Rev. Ramsey made a move to sit up but could not, his plight the same as those unfortunate insects whose accidentally crushed abdomens pinned the rest of them in place. Mr Haddington was pacing up and down the room.

'And then you, you pathetic old wreck, coming round here to patronise me.'

'It was only a social visit.'

'Oh you're awake are you. Still in the land of the living. I wish to God they'd drop the bomb, I wish to God they'd drop it tomorrow.' He bared his teeth and a fleck of saliva fell down his chin.

'Now Peter —'

'Yes. Yes. What is it?' said Mr Haddington, humming impatiently.

'You must make an effort to involve yourself in the local community you know,' began the vicar a little nervously. 'It's not good to shut yourself up day after day, writing or whatever. Out and about. Get out and about. Gardening. Enjoy the autumn of one's life. The labourer is worthy of his hire and his redundancy pay.' He made a small chuckling noise. 'Now's not really a time to worry oneself unnecessarily. Shouldn't allow these things to prey on your mind.'

Mr Haddington was sitting now quietly, his right hand resting on the small pile of his papers. His head had a narrow, defeated look. They sat for minutes without even the relief of a ticking clock. All the air in the room was quiet and empty. Dust and smoke from the fire rose steadily. They breathed in and out in a stilted way.

Evenly they were divided, one reconciled, the other not.

Mr Haddington picked up his papers and dropped them onto the coals.

'My dear boy,' said the vicar alarmed, 'should you have done that?'

Mr Haddington leant back his head and howled like a wolf, like a child.

The Selkie*

He came again that night not caring if he seemed a fool or was a fool. Other village men had dared each other to take the long night watch here, but none had stuck to it, none was as stubborn as he. For them it was half a joke, something to mock in loud uneasy voices. And he, what did he believe? Not that he could catch a Selkie, not that, but maybe he'd get a glimpse of one, that would be glory enough.

He settled down behind the usual rock wrapped in the overcoat, with a bottle of something to comfort himself with if the cold proved too much. High up the clouds were racing, it was a bad night for fishing, the air smelt deceitful. There'd be no one out this night. No one except himself and maybe the ones he was hoping for. He dreamt of them often. He did not know why.

*Selkies are people of the sea. In the water they go in the shape of seals, on the land their appearance is human. They live mostly in the Northern waters and are known to the island dwellers off the coast of Scotland.

Then finally when he saw, not one, but many, dancing the delicate boundary between land and water, he felt, he felt . . . It was either shock nor elation.

'It was the way they danced', he would say years later moving his hands quickly and slowly through the air before letting them drop. 'No not like that.'

He crawled gently forward, moving in time to the sudden scuts of wind and rain. From rock to rock he crept, his eyes fixed on them. He was praying, or something like praying. He felt the strain of a terrible effort, a taste of sickness in his mouth, sourness. The fear of failure, only yards from them, maddened him. Suddenly he tore upright from the ground and ran at them arms flailing. Perhaps he screamed. Then, as in his dreams, came something that left him frozen, motionless, on the seashore.

Hours he stood there unable to shift a bone, face fixed out to the black water. He thought nothing. He felt nothing. Not until the first crack of the sun did he stir and shake himself. His body was as cold as a corpse. If ever a man needed a drop he did. With hands as stiff and clumsy as stone he managed, after ten minutes, to get the bottle from his pocket. He unscrewed the cap and raised it up, spilling more on the coat than he poured into his mouth. He didn't mind, the very smell of the stuff was warm. He began banging his arms, stamping his feet, shaking out the bitter cramping cold. It was then he saw it, there, just under his left boot, he had stamped on it once already. It was the skin of a Selkie.

It was a miracle. It was a rush of joy warmer than any whiskey. He gathered the precious bundle in his arms and stumbling still with half thawed body, ran up and down the foreshore.

'Selkie!' he called out, 'Selkie I have you now,' he shouted. 'Selkie! he roared.

Then he paused and muttered to himself, 'Think man, think. If I was to come across her and I've the skin in my hand won't she just take it and go? I haven't my strength back yet. Hide it. Hide it before I find her. She cannot go back to the sea without her skin.'

Up to the small cave he went and hid it high in a small crevice he'd found and played in as a child. He didn't need to hurry himself now, he knew that what he wanted was his. Carefully he began his search down by the shore in rock pools and among the broken boulders. But it was up past the high tide mark he found her, asleep or maybe unconscious. He hardly paused to look at her but hoisted her up and over his shoulder and began the mile long trek to his hut. It was a hard journey. Sometimes she seemed to weigh less than a breath of air and other times was so heavy that he walked with his legs buckling and half crying with the pain.

He laid her down onto the bed and sat himself slowly on a chair to look at her. She seemed both less strange and more strange in such homely surroundings. There was a line with his socks drying, the bag of onions, the old carving of his father's and in the midst, on his bed, a Selkie plucked fresh from the sea. He took a short pull of whiskey to clear his head. Marvels and wonders, he toasted himself and laughed.

'By god she's naked.' Instinctively he turned his face. 'There's a blanket beneath you,' he said and waited for the sound of movement. 'There's a blanket, a blanket,' he spoke slowly, 'beneath you. Do you not understand?'

It was clear she did not. He glanced at her, her eyes were opening and closing, her hands clenching and un-clenching. He got up and went to the chest for something to put over her.

'You'll be cold, I expect. Cold,' he repeated. It was a bitter night. 'Here,' he said and dropped the cover over her. 'Wrap it round yourself now'. He smiled at her anxiously. 'There's no women here you know, just myself. I'll get a bit of a fire going in a while, don't worry. You'll be hungry maybe? Would you take a drop of this? Just to warm you?'

He offered her the bottle but she made no move. He felt a curious reluctance to touch her again. Her smell, not brine, not fish, not anything he could identify, made his eyes ache and the cold of her body numbed his fingers.

'Drink,' he said lifting the bottle to her lips. The liquid poured up to her mouth, at the first touch she screamed. He nearly dropped the bottle. 'What the hell,' he began and then he saw. All over her lips and wherever the whiskey had splashed on her were red ugly burn marks.

For him the next few months were exhausting. He was at times frustrated, amused, patient and impatient. Here was a woman without knowledge of any kind. Word by word he taught her, 'this is a chair, this is a net,' but she never took well to talking. There were strange things too, the way she tried to eat her food raw, her reluctance to stay in the house. It was heart-breaking trying to teach her to clean the hut, to cook the food. And she was clumsy, he couldn't trust her with the nets though the repairing of them was a shore job and her duty.

'What'll I call you then?' he asked. 'Jeannie was my mother's name, will I call you that? That's a compliment mind'.

Coming home from the day's fishing he would call out 'Jeannie, Jeannie I'm home'. She would get up from the rock in the nearby field where she spent most of the day and come to the house. One evening, for a joke almost, he called out, 'Marigold, Marigold,' and she came just as usual. It gave him a strange feeling that.

'Are you homesick? Are you missing the sea?' he asked one evening. 'Come we'll walk together down to the sea.' He took her by the arm and walked her down along the old chalk path. As they came to the last dip of land she stopped. 'Come on,' he roared. 'It's only a step more. Ah it's a wild night tonight, there'll be a great storm tonight.'

As far as the sand he got her but not further. She looked at the savage water with incomprehension or maybe just blankly. The fisherman dragged her home cursing and angry.

'Are you pretending to me? Do you remember nothing? You're more witless than a beast. Do you not remember how I rescued you from that place, how I carried you home? Without me where are you? Where is your gratitude girl?'

He took her to the village once only. The old priest, with a hard look on his face, married them in the side chapel. The village was as busy as on a market day, men, women and children all came out to see the stranger.

'A fine catch you got there,' shouted a young fellow which set some of them laughing.

And for the Selkie how did it seem? How was your life in the crust of stone the man called a house? How was this world without depth or height where you could move only step by step on the hard ungiving earth? Did you remember soaring high and light in the shallows or plunging down into the heavy weight of the dark? Did you remember the broken green of the sun? The sweet bitter taste of living fish? The air you breathed here was it tasteless and dry, was it like choking on ashes?

Every day before he left the house the fisherman lit the fire from last night's embers. She would sit in the furthest corner watching it licking itself into flames. She must go soon and put the cauldron with spring water, oats and salt on the hook over the hearth. This was a thing she must do every morning. There it was flickering and chattering like a mad thing in its circle of stone. It hurt even to look at and as she went towards it carrying the heavy pot, red welts came up on her white body and she was near to fainting. All day it lived in the house and she must feed it with wood and peat. Even in the night it glowed at her heavy with dust and ashes. The man would speak to it as a friend, it welcomed him, but her it hated. Why else did it watch and whisper at her, what stories did it tell the man who was so often angry?

The years went by. It was a hard life, work and sleep made up the best part of the time. She had learned at last to do the things he wanted, the cooking, the mending of nets, all her wifely duties. There were times he was restless.

'Come Jeannie, won't you sing to me?' he asked pouring himself another half glass. 'Or dance maybe?

Who'd have thought I'd have ended up by having only a miserable mewling woman for my company?' He half smiled and waited for a reply.

The time came when he went down to the village to fetch the midwife there. She asked him little but made him wait while she went to the house of a neighbour. He carried her leather bag and they trudged the four miles to his hut. She was there all that night and the next day. It was evening when the two of them stood in the doorway, the midwife holding the new born girl child in her arms.

'It was hard for her bearing the child,' she said at last.

'So it seemed'.

'She's beautiful enough, I grant you that,' she said glancing back into the house.

'She's mine whatever she is,' he said.

'It's a hard matter though to keep such a creature. She's done you no harm it seems and now you have the child. Will you not give her back what's hers and let her go to her home?'

'There's no one she belongs to but me,' he said, 'and now there's a child.'

'I'd love now to see it. Would you let me see the Selkie skin as a reward for my trouble here?,' she bent closer with an eager expression on her face.

'I'll pay you,' he said.

'You're a fool man,' she said and bent down to rummage in her bag. She brought out a battered metal bottle. 'It may not be the freshest I grant you but it's woman's milk, the mistress next door is weaning still and didn't begrudge me this drop'.

'What's it for?' he asked bewildered.

'For the child. The child must taste woman's milk first.' She smiled at him. 'Do you want it to be like its mother?'

Three more times the Selkie was in childbirth and at the last she bore a son. The fisherman was pleased. He loved his daughter but looked to the future and wanted a son of his own to have his nets and his boat and not the husband of the girl.

They grew up in that rocky valley that swarmed with streams. The solitude they didn't notice. It was a natural thing that their father was out on the good days fishing and when the weather was bad mending his boat. When they were able to understand he explained to them that their mother came from over the water and that her ways were not the ways of the people hereabouts. He didn't want them playing with the children from the village. 'Stay close to the house', he ordered. 'I don't want the pair of you getting lost and I want you,' he said to the girl, 'I want you to keep an eye on,' he nodded his head in their mother's direction.

Once, or maybe they imagined it, the children woke in the night and saw the door of the house wide open. They crept out afraid and anxious. There on a rock in the nearby field was their mother. What was she doing? She had her face to the sea and there she danced and sang. The dancing was swift and very strange and the music seemed to freeze their bones. They ran back to the house and both of them hid their heads under the pillows.

The children loved the sea, though their father was sometimes angry if they went down to the cove too often. They played games there as long as the day itself. There was one time, it was the summer and they had been swimming each one in their favourite rock pool. 'Hide and seek. Hide and seek,' shouted the boy and ran off as his sister began to count. She opened her eyes when she finished. The boy was easy to find as he only ever hid in one of six places. She had got only as far as the overhanging rock, number four, when he came running up.

'I was in the cave.' He was breathless. 'I was in the cave, the big cave and I was finding a new place.'

'But we're not supposed to go there.'

'I was there,' he said, 'and I found this ledge high, high up. I was climbing and I found this ledge and there was something on the ledge.'

'And what was it?'

'I don't know. Come on. Come on.'

They ran along the beach and then up into the cave.

'It's very heavy,' he said up in the darkness. 'Careful now while I drop it down to you.'

They dragged it out onto the beach. They must have stared at it for over a minute. It lay there smooth to the touch but the colour of hard rock. The boy looked frightened.

'What is it? he asked.

They went home that evening quiet and made little noise during the evening meal. The fisherman came home late after a poor catch and so it was as well to be silent. He hunched close to the fire, smoking and taking his drop.

The next morning they played near home, in the field, building dams across the streams, trying to find an echo off a nearby hill. The were aware of their mother sitting on her rock, her eyes following the flight of the gulls.

'Come on,' said the girl rushing up to her suddenly. 'Come on, I found something yesterday, come and see.'

'It was me that found it,' said the boy.

'Never mind that now.'

Catching either hand the children pulled her off the rock and began running with her towards the shore. But onto the beach she would not go.

'I tell you what,' said the girl. 'I'll keep her here and you drag it up.'

'It's too heavy,' said the boy.

'It is not,' she gave him a shove, 'and hurry.'

When the boy came back the two of them struggled to open the bundle out onto the grass. They stood back and watched their mother.

'It's a present,' said one of the children. 'It's yours'.

They watched her kneel down and saw how she felt the smooth sleek shape of it with her hands. They heard the crooning, wailing sound she made with her head thrown back and her mouth open. They watched her kneeling there, her body struggling against her.

She was looking at them.

'Children,' she said.

The boy stood kicking the stones on the pathway.

'Don't,' whispered the girl to him.

She kept looking at them in a way that made them feel strange, as though they were strange, unaccountable. As if she was fascinated, as if she was drawn to them. All the time her back was against the sea, her body still now, but the eyes wild as it cried and called for her.

'Go on,' one of them said. 'Go on,' they both said.

She got to her feet somehow, the bundle clutched up in her arms.

'Go on' they shrieked, 'Quickly, go on.'

Then slowly, slowly like a creature dazed by good fortune or loss, she walked down to the beach over the rocks and the sand. She stood at the water's margin and they heard her shout something in a human voice. Then the Selkie went back to the sea.

Flights of Angels

She wakes up at the rattle of the tea trolley, to the taste of boiled glue in her mouth. By the time her eyelashes are ungummed pain has slid its vivid fingers across her chest and begun to grip. Every morning it comes, quick as consciousness and more eager. She turns her head and looks as she does every morning, through the high hospital window at the relaxed unbounded blue of the early morning sky.

'This, you call this, what?' demands the voice of the Signora.

'It's a cup of tea, that's what it is,' says the nurse.

'Tea-pee-piss. Oh yes. I know what this is, exactly. What is the problem with coffee I ask?'

'I've explained before —'

'And where is my wig?' asks the Signora.

'Your wig is in your locker. You know perfectly well where your wig is. And you don't need it now. You have your own hair to manage,' replies the nurse.

'My wig needs to be combed. And this stuff,' the Signora yanks at a handful of her hair, 'this isn't hair.

This is not my hair.'

'I'm not going to argue the point with you', says the nurse, beginning to move away.

'Good. Go and fetch my breakfast.'

Mrs Jeffries hears the dip and clank of the tea trolley moving steadily down the ward and towards her. She would pay pounds to have the wheels, or the castors, or whatever makes that dreadful noise, oiled into silence.

'Well you're wide awake,' says the nurse, scooping her up and plumping the pillow behind her. 'You're in the best place, it's bitter out there, believe me.'

'Thank you.' The heat of the tea floods her mouth and she swallows away the aftertaste of last night's drugs.

'Not too much sugar?' asks Nurse Collins, and Mrs Jeffries lies and shakes her head.

From here until the arrival of breakfast are her fifteen beautiful minutes. In the bed her body comes clear of that heavy induced sleep and the pain hasn't gathered to its full strength. It hums, it hums still far from a crescendo. Fifteen beautiful minutes until breakfast and the relentlessness of pain and then the pain killers. What colour is that opaque and restful blue, out there outside, outside the window?

Women's Surgical has fifteen beds, seven down one side, eight the other. There are side wards, small rooms past sister's office, only one of these is occupied by a Mrs Lawton unseen by the rest of the patients but audible unfortunately. Mrs Jeffries has tried to remember the people who have occupied the various beds around her. Mrs Morgan who'd worked in motor insurance for twenty-nine years, was still here. There was the woman with the kidney, and listless Lisa wandering up and down the ward, — the Signora of course. They were all here from before her operation, that's how she knew them. All the others were strangers. Now, they told her, she was to concentrate on getting well. It was easier to concentrate on the pain, it required her concentration, demanded it, and she was grateful for the escape it offered.

It was eggs again. Boiled eggs for breakfast.

'This you see,' says the Signora, 'is the spoon and this is the egg. I hit it, so, on the head. This is my head and crunch goes the shell. And then I slice the top of my head off.' She peers curiously into the egg.

Mrs Morgan says to the new patient on her left, 'They've told her not to do that you know. They may as well talk to the wall as that one.'

'Very, very soon you'll see. Bang, crunch, scoop.' The Signora's face puckers, she waves her spoon at Mrs Jeffries.

'I wish they didn't wake us so early. It makes the day seem so long,' Mrs Morgan says across to her new friend, who murmurs something in reply. It is a rule of Mrs Morgan's never to start knitting until her breakfast things are cleared away, it is a rule she adheres to strictly. Then the clink of her knitting needles would seem to summon forth the drug trolley from its locked cupboard and conjure it up the ward.

'That's no good is it,' says Staff Nurse to Mrs Jeffries, her uneaten breakfast on display, 'How do you expect to get well?'

'I'm sorry.'

'If you don't fancy the eggs, you can always eat the toast. That's how we get infections — not eating enough. That's how they get worse.'

Briefly Mrs Jeffries imagines Staff Nurse drowned in the bottom of a ditch.

'You must have something in your stomach before you take a pill. Always. Prevents indigestion.' She frowns. 'Come on now, try.'

So Mrs Jeffries sucks at the end of a piece of toast while the water is poured into a small beaker. The beaker is put on the locker. She swallows the mouthful she has, then another, then one more, all round the crust.

'There,' says Staff Nurse.

The capsules cover half the palm of her hand. She stares at them with the depressed avidity of an addict. I am an addict, I'd kill for these, she thinks.

The day has started, the needles click, the querulous

voices complain. Lisa begins her endless, aimless wanderings, there are bed baths and bad pans, chat, the crisp squeak of rubber-soled shoes, rumours and the recital of bowel movements and immobilities. Mrs Jeffries abandons it all, she is neutral. She watches impartially the contest in her body, the old opponent, pain, in the red corner, and out of the blue arises the dazzling fugg of a half-coma. She slips under the ropes, her jaws slacken.

. . . And there, riding over her left shoulder, the heavy hooves of the French hussars. It is war, it is war. The infantry wheel in confusion, obscured by smoke, and shouting in strange languages. Seconds pass between the flash of fire and the explosion of shells through the German ranks, knocking them down like ninepins. Why ninepins? A terrified horse screams, deadlocked in clay. There are orders and trumpets and furious clashes with lumps of turf tearing up, falling down. They light fires on the hill signalling for reinforcements. Who signals? It's cold, it's bitter and the blood steams as it pours out of wounds and mouths, over uniforms, everywhere. And now they drag the heavy artillery across and over her stomach and pound into the hills where the generals are hiding. Bald and burnt they are, bald and burnt, nothing growing, not a thing — a blade of grass? The sheets wind round her body breathlessly and they have only six miles to go before they can enter Paris. Paris starves and waits, there is nothing left, the rats are eaten and the rich are in Normandy.

What is she doing here, why is she lying here with these armies, these fighting men, chopping and cutting and killing, burning, burning all over — all over what? The ground. But surely this body is a strange choice for a battlefield. There must be sómewhere else, a more suitable place, to fight the 1870 Franco-Prussian War. She is too small, the wrong shape. That's obvious, she thinks, as she wakes up in the ward and looks down at a body as flat as folded linen.

'Time we changed those dressings,' says Staff Nurse. 'I'll do it today I think. Nurse Collins is a good worker but a bit heavy handed. You slept through lunch. '

'I'm sorry.'

'I want you to have a bit of fruit after we've finished this. Will you undress yourself or will I?'

Mrs Jeffries' hands are dull and tired and give up after the second button. 'Half asleep,' she says, 'we could leave it till later.'

But the nurse smiles, her name tag is pinned over her right breast. Mrs Jeffries looks firmly at the clipboard at the bottom of her bed. She holds a piece of her cheek between her teeth. And as the last flimsy piece of dressing peels away and she wants to open her mouth and whimper and curse, down she bites but there's only the faint taste of blood.

'That's what I call a sluggish wound,' says Staff Nurse. 'You're taking your time. Still paining a lot I expect?'

Mrs Jeffries would like the ceiling to crash down and crush them both into pulp, real pulp.

'It's a very serious operation. ' This sternly, nodding her head, once, twice. 'Still . . . ' She concentrates on the new dressing. 'Poor Mrs Kelleher's going fast.'

'Mrs Kelleher?'

'Her opposite — she's been opposite you this last week poor soul. Mind you if you're in your eighties you can't expect to carry on forever. The family have a pub somewhere out of town, not the country exactly but on the road out. Left to the daughter I understand. She's married.'

'Could I have a drink, have a drink of water?' says Mrs Jeffries.

'You certainly can — and an orange too. And if you take a couple of biscuits I'll be able to give you your pain-killers, won't I?'

'Yes.'

It is easy to envy old Mrs Kelleher with the drip in her arm, like a plant she is bathed in a regular flow of nutriments, put under glass and left to her own devices. Yet somehow Mrs Jeffries does not like to look at her.

'Bloody bitches, where is my doctor?' shouts the Signora.

Malcolm appears just as Mrs Jeffries has finished swallowing her pills. He appears abruptly, like a apparition — out of context. He is the first visitor of the day and comes bearing flowers. He tries a jaunty walk down the ward as all the women watch him. For a second or two he looks down at her then bends and kisses her cheek.

'What'll I do with these?' he asks, waving the chrysanthemums. 'I'll stick 'em in here for the moment?'' He undoes the wrapping paper carefully and puts the flowers in the water jug.

'How are you? The kids?'

'Fine, fine. I'll take my coat off. God it's like a furnace in here.' He drops the overcoat at the bottom of the bed, across her feet. 'How are you feeling?'

'Oh you know . . .'

'Sister was saying,' he takes hold of her hand and begins counting her fingers absently.

'They're all there. My fingers.'

'What?' he asks not following her, but letting her hand go anyway.

At 45 Malcolm is a distinctly handsome man. He is boyish in a way she sometimes likes and sometimes finds ridiculous. He has the ingenuous habit of looking directly into the eyes of anyone he is addressing to impress them with his honesty and sincerity. It was a habit that is costing him now.

'You're not to worry. It's early days yet and Sister was saying there's every chance in the world that — she says you're not eating, that you're fretting. We're managing fine at home, there's nothing to worry you for a minute on that score.'

The weight of his coat is extraordinary, incredible — it's as though casts of concrete have been placed on her feet and any second the pressure will cause her ankles to snap. What was it made of, why had he put it there? It is hurting her.

'Did you bring the photographs?'

'I forgot,' he lied.

'I want to see them Malcolm.'

'OK. I won't forget next time, but I don't want you getting upset.'

Into the silence she says, 'I had a dream about the war.'

'You're too young to remember the war.'

She could think of nothing more to say. The weight of the coat exhausts her. It is a millstone and she is falling down, drowning in some wide lake, a desolate place. She can hear the lost cry of birds from the reedbed, the crack of guns and the voice of her father shouting swim, swim over here, over to the boat you silly girl. She's so tired and besides her wellingtons are full of water. It is too late, they weigh a ton. And then just like a miracle because she has made no effort, no appeal, the boots fall off and down they drop. Relief is exquisite. It is the most exquisite thing.

'Malcolm,' she whispers. The chair is empty. The coat is gone. 'Malcolm.'

'You've been asleep. He's not here. He's gone,' says Lisa with her hands on the windowsill and not turning round. Seagulls fly past from the city dump and out to the sea. 'Looks bloody miserable out there, doesn't it?'

Mrs Jeffries pushes herself a little more upright.

'You want anything? Tea?' asks Lisa. 'They'll bring it round soon. Day really drags out doesn't it.' She hums and begins walking back up the ward, her slippers slopping off at every step.

She doesn't like it up here, thinks Mrs Jeffries, not with the old woman comatose on the drip and me, and me — but it's the only window on the ward. She looks out but everything is scattered, fragmentary, roads, buildings, bushes all jumbled, nothing unique. And as it gets darker, as time passes, she begins to see the reflection, insubstantial at first, of the old woman opposite. There's even a hint of that curious overused yellow of her skin, the smudges of brown under eyes like ghostly nicotine. We are both eyesores, bedsores, she thinks, a little amused, and shifts her bottom to one side. The sheet is momentarily tugged tight across her chest and then like scissors, like scalding, like branding, unlike anything but itself — pain possesses her.

Coming through the swing doors is the tea trolley propelled by Nurse Collins.

'Nurse,' says Mrs Jeffries, 'these painkillers, they're not enough, they're not working. I can't rest. I can't eat with this pain. I want to get better. I do. I do!' The soft tears of self-pity leak across the side of her head and into her hair.

Nurse Collins brings the ham salad, she smiles at Mrs Jeffries. 'Will I plump those pillows up for you?' she asks, and puts the plates down as she does so. 'And we could do with plumping you up while we're at it. Everything OK, want anything?'

'Nothing.'

Now the day can wind down. The able-bodied go into the ward room to watch television. Mrs Morgan is established in the high-backed chair with her knitting in hand and her new friend on the left. Lisa leans on the doorway unwilling to commit herself and the Signora sits in bed with her reading glasses on.

In the centre of the ward, three nurses are in consultation. As a body they turn and walk up the ward towards Mrs Jeffries. She chews frantically on the limp frill of a lettuce leaf but it's not her they want. They pull the curtains all the way round the old lady opposite. All the way round, but the window side is left open. Staring ahead Mrs Jeffries can only see the floral pattern of the curtain material, but looking to her left she can see reflected in the window quite another story.

'Mrs Kelleher, Mrs Kelleher, can you hear me?' asks Staff Nurse. 'We have to relieve some of the pressure on your bladder, do you understand me. Now we've tried popping you up on the bedpan but that hasn't worked so I'm afraid we'll have to give you a little help.' The bedclothes come back. 'Here, can you see, Jen?' She puts the tube on the locker for a moment.

After about fifteen minutes the curtains swing back.

The younger nurse looks frustrated and upset, the old lady looks just as she always does, her head dwarfed by the over-supplied fruit bowl. They hadn't been very success-ful. Mrs Jeffries feels almost awake. Her eyes burn, time passes. Just before lights out she's surprised to see Signora sitting on her visitor's chair.

'A visitor,' explains the Signora, holding her upended wig in her hands.

They sit in silence for a few minutes.

'Where are you from?' asks Mrs Jeffries.

The Signora glances over her shoulder at her bed.

'I mean what part of Italy.'

'Italy? Italy?' says the Signora puzzled. 'Last week you, this week me, that's what it is.'

'Are you, are you worried about the operation?'

The Signora shrugs. 'I'm sick and tired, that's what it is.' She gives Mrs Jeffries a long look. 'Well.'

'I don't follow you?'

'You don't follow me?'

'No.'

'I follow you then.'

'I hope not,' says Mrs Jeffries quietly.

'No?' The Signora turns the wig between the palms of her hands. 'A pity.'

'Bedtime I'm afraid ladies,' says Nurse Collins.

'Bloody bitch,' says the Signora.

'Takes one to know one I suppose, eh Mrs Jeffries,' Nurse Collins says in jovial humour.

As she watches the Signora's exaggerated unsteady progress back to her bed, Mrs Jeffries tries to regain the threads of her thoughts. Tonight, she decides, I will not take the painkillers, I will not take the sleeping tablets. I will stay steady, I will stay sober. I'm getting so careless, I don't care, it can't continue. So when Nurse Collins returns rattling her pills in that tiny dice cup she says, 'I'll take them in a minute.'

'Who put the flowers in the water jug?' clicks Nurse Collins. 'We'll have to borrow some water from your next door neighbour.' She pours a full expert glass and hands it over to Mrs Jeffries.

'I'll take them in a minute.'

'Just pop them down,' advises nurse.

'In a minute.'

'Have to have you settled for the nightstaff you see.'

She is sucked slowly back into thick, dreaming collapse as the bricks fly out of the walls and the bonfires are seen everywhere in old and new ruins alike. For miles she drags her heavy bags, not lost exactly but recognising only in glimpses the districts she walks through. A dog pads and pants steadily behind her, an ulcer on one of its forelegs. She hates it, she wants to rest, to lie down, to put these parcels in the rubble and lie down with them. Over to the right a big brass swinging ball has cleared half a house. On the top storey a young girl watches the ball rising up towards her. Her mouth is open, she is dancing with delight as the walls crash down around her. There is a sound of the metal, the bunching of chain as it sweeps back to sweep forward. This is a nightmare, thinks Mrs Jeffries. The girl is not invulnerable but she is not afraid, it must be a nightmare.

The metal is still jarring when she wakes up, her head turns involuntarily towards the window. There is movement, she can see the reflection of movement but hardly any sound except the squeak and clank of a trolley Voices are kept very low at this time of night. It is the worst thing in the world to wake the ward up. For a while she can't make out what's happening, then she sees the metal box on its six shining castors being wheeled away. It is Mrs Kelleher. Mrs Jeffries recognises that coffin. Now the bed opposite is free, the drip dangles, half-empty and unattached. Almost before it has time to happen it's over and done with. The bedclothes are bundled up and carried off. Tomorrow they will say Mrs Kelleher has passed away peacefully. It is a peace that passes Mrs Jeffries' understanding.

For the next three long hours she watches them make their night patrol every half-hour. As they come to her she is at pains to make the sounds of someone comfortably asleep. She doesn't think, not deliberately. Images and memories come and go as they please, not connecting, not coming to any conclusions, just as they happen to happen. She could wait, she must wait, fighting the long defeat against pain and sleep. At five o'clock the light will have shimmered through and that she will accept as both signal and release. She must stay awake.

She wakes up with that fear of having overslept, having missed the exam, the interview, but no, for once she is lucky. There is time, still time, the window's square blackness has only just begun to loosen. It is a luxury to lie so calmly, so in control. Then for the first time since the operation she sits up and swings her legs out of the bed. There is no time to look at them and see their yellowed-out suntan, to regret her thin chicken-skinned scrag of a body. She stands up, clutching the windowsill for a hand-hold as now she must hurry, hurry to open the window wide, letting the light in and letting the air escape. There are six, seven, stories between her and the ground. She hitches the nightdress up and over her head, despite the pain, because it is important to take nothing, not one thing, with her. She even unpins the bandages, but it will take too long to unravel them. It is very cold perched on the windowsill, and ugly. She hears the voices behind her. Now it is time to let go, launch out. There is air all around her, light everywhere and from her body the bright white banners are flying.

Duelling Scars

The funeral was worse than Mrs Gorman could have imagined. She had prepared herself to offer no response to the reek and clatter of the censer, the embroidered vestments; she was even ready to genuflect, cross herself and pray aloud when and where appropriate. Don, after all, had been a Catholic of a sort and it was only right that he have a Catholic funeral. At least the service was no longer in Latin, she had comforted herself beforehand, at least she'd know what was going on. In the event it would have been better if it had been in any language under the sun other than English. Never had Mrs Gorman encountered such barbaric sentiments: blood, blood, blood, intoned the priest, corruption and death. It was like something out of the Congo. It was extraordinary. It was disgusting. The man didn't even know Don.

'God, isn't it a pity that Lizzie isn't here,' whispered an obscure cousin of Don's as they made their way across the carpark. 'She'll be breaking her heart, her own daddy's funeral, and her stuck unable to get a flight, all that way over there in Melbourne.'

'Sydney,' said Mrs Gorman, taking deep breaths of the clear, fine air. She had the sensation of having been trapped in some asphyxiating box. She gave the building behind her a cold look.

'Sydney,' said the cousin agreeably. 'It's a lovely day at least. I don't know if that's worse or better.'

Martin, Don's senior by fifteen years, patted her knee all the way to the cemetery. It was impossible to tell if his pale grey eyes had been stung by the wind or if he was weeping. His lower lip was very moist. Cissy, his wife, kept a packet of paper handkerchiefs in her hand and her gaze fixed mournfully on Mrs Gorman's face. Mrs Gorman wished she'd insisted on travelling alone.

'A grand man,' said Martin heavily. Mrs Gorman made no reply. Martin shook her head. 'A grand chap. One of the very best, though he was my brother.'

'Well, at least he didn't suffer,' said Casey who'd made that remark before.

'There's a lot of traffic on the road,' said Mrs Gorman.

Martin made a gesture with his head as though he was about to look out the window but he kept his face turned to her. 'Don't you worry, don't you fret. We'll be there, we'll get there.'

'It'll be over soon enough. You could do with a cup of tea, a nice hot cup of tea,' suggested Cissy.

'Or something stronger,' Martin said kindly.

'Or something stronger, whatever you wish.'

'Thank you,' said Mrs Gorman.

They lapsed into silence.

His hand on her knee was stained with tobacco and the veins stood out like frayed blue flex.

The same priest led the service at the graveside, his wispy old body held carefully against the wind, perhaps there was a regulation against wearing overcoats when officiating, Mrs Gorman speculated. With canvas bands underneath the coffin they lowered Don. Then someone came at Mrs Gorman with a container of holy water. She sprinkled liquid into the open hole and onto the hard brown varnish of the lid. There was a similar thing to be done with a handful of earth.

When it was over and the flowers had been set aside for delivery to the local hospital, she found herself being escorted back to the car. There she stood in her matt-black suit shaking hands with all comers. People peered at her, squeezed her hands, arms, murmured comfort, condolences, assurance of assistance. It was like being a public figure suddenly. Row after row of bone-coloured monuments disappeared off in all directions. The wind was particularly cutting.

Martin and Cissy had repeatedly offered the use of their house for ' a drop and a bite afterwards' . Naturally Mrs Gorman would not hear of it. She had five large plates of sandwiches cut, there would be tea for the ladies, whiskey for the gentlemen. She had even bought some bottles of beer for the younger men though it seemed to be an inappropriate drink for such an event. She wasn't sure she liked either of Cissy and Martin's boys, though they were hardly boys, being grown men with families of their own. Still they persisted in maintaining some of the trapping of surly adolescence. Raymond, in particular, always referred to her as 'missus' in a tone and an accent she suspected.

Putting her key in the door Mrs Gorman was conscious of a familiar prickle of pride in her lovely home. There could be no question that it was something to be proud of, individual, without the use of lurid colours or prodigies of futuristic furniture design.

'It's a lovely house,' sighed Cissy sympathetically.

Mrs Gorman looked at her. It was hard to understand how anyone could let herself go like that. Her chin for instance slipped like a half-set blancmange into the fold of her neck and disappeared. She persisted in wearing purple and dark red, neither of which was at all suitable for a woman with high blood pressure. At least today she was in black.

She moved into the kitchen to switch on the already filled kettle and to take off the dampened cloths covering the plates of sandwiches. Noreen, Raymond's wife, came in to assist but really it was quicker to manage by herself.

The people present in the main were relatives of Don's and therefore, by extension, relatives of hers she supposed. One or two neighbours had popped in and there was a small knot of Don's friends from the old days. These stood together between the sandwiches and the sideboard.

'You'll take a drop,' Martin insisted from across the room.

'To warm you,' said Cissy.

A cut-glass tumbler made its way over to her in the hand of a young girl Mrs Gorman could not remember having seen before.

'I'm Mary,' said the girl blushing. 'I'm Noreen's sister. She's married to Ray,'continued the girl, her face suffused with colour. 'Will I get you a sandwich or something?'

'No thank you,' said Mrs Gorman. As she turned to put the tumbler on the television a middle-aged man with a maroon jumper taut over his belly managed to catch her eye.

'Don was a great footballer in his young days you know.'

'Yes?'

'Yes, he was,' said the man. 'That was a long time ago mark you. Young rips we were then.' He looked at her expectantly.

All around her people began to relax, unbutton their jackets, to help themselves to another drink and abandon the pretence of the teacup. There was even laughter from the group of men still holding firm between the sideboard and the depleting plate of sandwiches.

'Bottle opener?' whispered the young girl, carrying a large bottle of Guinness in her hands. She smiled nervously.

'I'm sorry?'

'Aunty Cissy said she'd looked through the sideboard. She went through every drawer. And we couldn't find one.'

'Find what?'

'A bottle opener,' she whispered, and her mouth hung open like a wound-down toy.

At that moment the telephone rang. Immediately the room became serious and silent. It rang on and on like an animal caught in the monotony of pain.

'That'll be Lizzie,' said Cissy loudly.

'Will I answer it for her?' Martin inquired.

'Get on and answer it, supposing it rang off,' somebody else advised her, a neighbour who'd clearly enjoyed the benefits of Martin's generous measures. 'Come on now Rose.' She nudged Mrs Gorman into motion.

Mrs Gorman sat down in front of the coffee table with the televison facing her. She could see a grey middle-aged woman swimming or drowning in its depths. 'Hello, ' she said into the receiver.

There was a far away ping, relatives craned forward, ready with encouragement.

'Hello,' said a voice. 'Hello Mum?'

'Oh send her all our loves,' said Cissy, bent nearly double with the pressure of her emotions.

Mrs Gorman put the receiver carefully back in its cradle. 'Wrong number,' she announced. She felt the disappointment flow through the room, almost enjoyed it.

'That's a shame,' said Noreen.

'Are you sure now it wasn't Lizzie?' asked Raymond.

'She'd know her own daughter's voice,' said Noreen, her nose beaked forward aggressively.

'I was only asking a question,' said her husband. He had managed to open his beer bottle without an opener. He drained his glass. 'I was asking a question and it wasn't you I was asking. Right, missus?'

Briskly Mrs Gorman went over to the table and began clearing it. She didn't care that she was stacking plates of half-eaten, even uneaten sandwiches one on top of another.

'He wouldn't have wanted us to grieve,' said a man

in a blue lanky suit. Every tooth in his mouth was crooked. He put a hand on her arm.

'I was just going through to the kitchen with these, ' replied Mrs Gorman.

'He had a good life. He had great luck over there, made his money, had a home and family. And he died here at home in Ireland. There's not much more a man can ask.'

'You'll excuse me.'

'I'm a friend of Martin's you understand, but I knew your Don. I knew him well in the old days. The days that are dead and gone. If you ever need a hand with your wiring, Sean Whelan's your man.' He smiled kindly.

'I must get these in the sink,' she said, easing past.

Once in the kitchen she scraped every last scrap from the plates into the dustbin, noisily with a clean knife. The hot water gushed into the sink and the washing-up liquid squeaked aloud when she squeezed it in. One by one she cleaned the plates. She could see through the window the beginning of neglect in the garden.

Raymond and Cissy were in the doorway. 'A few of the people are going, neighbours. Martin can see them off if you like,' said Cissy.

'I'll tell Noreen to come in and give you a hand with those dishes,' Raymond offered.

'There's no need.' Mrs Gorman felt she had had the same expression clamped on her face for hours. 'I'm finished.'

Back in the lounge all but the closest relatives had left or were leaving. Ray and Noreen's youngest was asleep on the settee. Mrs Gorman wondered what they were giving that child: it was always asleep. Martin came over and, cupping his hand under her elbow, led her over to one of the armchairs. He stood in front of her and began.

'Rose, there's something I want to have you understand.' He looked round the room, everyone was paying attention. 'Charles here will bear me out.'

'And Raymond,' Cissy put in.

'And Raymond,' conceded Martin. 'It's just this.

Now only time will heal the grief. That's understood. We all understand that. But there's something you have to know. We're a family. There's been ups and downs, but we're a family. Don was my brother and you are his wife and that means we're all a family, all of us gathered here today on this sad occasion.' Martin's eyes glistened. Mrs Gorman sat with her two hands holding one another. ' Rose, Rose, ' he said.

'Any help,' prompted Cissy.

'Any help, advice, or assistance at any time, day or night. Just pick up that phone,' he pointed at the phone.

That young girl Mary was handing out pieces of fruit-cake on her clean plates. On the table there was a large plastic cakebox with a red lid.

'I thought a bit of fruitcake might come in handy. Ballast,' Cissy said. 'It's homemade.' She tilted her head to one side, her cakes were always justly praised.

'I'm very tired,' said Mrs Gorman. 'I think I'll go upstairs and lie down.'

'You do that. You just do that. You lie down and have a bit of peace and quiet,' said Cissy, getting up and preparing to accompany her sister-in-law. While she was hunting under her chair for her handbag, Mrs Gorman saw her opportunity and escaped. Once upstairs she sat on the bed and let the relief of being alone rush in on her. The voices downstairs were getting less inhibited.

'They'll be dancing next,' said Mrs Gorman grimly. ' Or singing. Or both.'

She slipped off her shoes and was about to lie down when she thought better of it. Better to lock the door. It was possible Cissy could force her way in here. She lay back on the counterpane and fought her way resolutely to sleep.

Even in sleep her face and body kept to their firm outlines, there was no slackening into flabbiness. She had kept her figure, a little thickened, a bit more braced but the essentials remained. She had always been an attractive woman and she had no intention of letting herself go. Hers was a strong framed and featured body that would see her comfortably through. It was well over a thousand years since her ancestors had raided then settled in the North of England, but no amount of intermarriage had lessened Rose Fairchild's Nordic good looks. Any horn-helmeted, axe wielding seafaring Viking would have known her for one of his own people. In appearance at least; the temperament had undergone some changes in the intervening centuries. Living within the conventions had always seemed to her both natural and necessary. If she was to look back over her life the only thing she would have to account for, her only eccentricity, was her marriage to Don.

Halifax. She had first met Don in Halifax. There was a new club and a whole gang of them were there, all pals, all talking and singing along to the lyrics. Don always said she was wearing a floral-print dress with a wide red belt clinched into her waist, but she didn't remember. She didn't remember either how it was that she ended up dancing with this tall thin young man, with the face of a camel, Jimmy her ex used to say. The progress of their courtship was comfortable and relaxed, there was never a man more tactful than Don. Even her parents were pleased by the engagement though he was Irish and a Catholic. Of course some of her relatives wouldn't come to the wedding and none of his did, except Martin, who was bestman. It was while they were signing the register that she discovered his real name was Donal not Donald as she'd always assumed. He used to tease her about that, saying to their friends that the poor girl didn't know who she was marrying.

'I was marrying the man, not the name,' she'd reply crisply.

Martin had been a bit put out that they were married in a Protestant church, but that was Don's decision. She'd made it plain that, if Don wanted, she'd go to the local Catholic church and do whatever was necessary. The brothers had argued about that, but Don was right, he was what they call lapsed and it would have been just hypocrisy he said. Secreily she was grateful, especially after a few years when she got pregnant. It was one thing to be married to a Catholic, it was quite another to be the mother of one, she said to her own mother.

She was in labour for what felt like weeks and months. She had been confident, given her strong and healthy body, that she'd be out of the labour ward almost before she was in. She lay on the sweat and blood stained sheet, pushing and heaving like a ship straining to pull from shore and out into the open sea. When at last half-delirious with gas and exhaustion they had managed to deliver the baby she was past the point of caring. The baby lay in a cot at the side of the bed, small, pink, delicate and unnaturally quiet. Mrs Gorman couldn't connect the pain her body had undergone with this aloof and separate individual. Lizzie would be an only child they both agreed.

Don did very well with his electrical supply shop. Within ten years he owned two branches in the town and was the exclusive stockist and distributor in the area for one of the larger British companies. He surprised everybody. He had none of the bullying self-congratulatory shrewdness of the Yorkshire businessman, but then neither did he have that plausible roguish charm that might have been expected from an Irishman.

Mrs Gorman would have been the first to say that there was little to complain of in those years, indeed they were happy times.

Then one Sunday when Lizzie was a grown girl of eighteen and they were all sitting down to the roast-lamb dinner, Don announced that he was selling up the business and going home.

'Home?' said Rose.

'Ireland,' said Don. 'It's about time I did.' He picked up his fork and went on calmly eating his dinner. But Rose Gorman was no fool, she was quick enough to catch the look that passed between Don and her daughter. They had discussed this behind her back.

She didn't storm at him, she didn't scream and shout, that wasn't her style, and besides she couldn't be expected to treat this seriously. Never in all the years of their marriage had he mentioned going to Ireland except for a holiday. They had gone twice together.

'Martin'll find us somewhere to live until I can look about.' Don pulled down his habitually rucked cardigan, trying to anchor it over his narrow hips. He stood in the doorway, clearly intending to go upstairs for his Sunday lie down.

'Don't talk nonsense,' said Rose. 'How can you talk such nonsense. This is our home, this is where we live. Besides,' she said. 'Lizzie isn't going to get a job over there, there aren't jobs there.'

'That doesn't matter,' said Lizzie.

'Of course it matters,' snapped Rose.

'When I'm finished training I won't be staying in this part of the world anyway. I'll probably go to Saudi Arabia.'

'Lizzie . . .' said her mother.

'Or Australia. More likely Australia.' She laughed and Mrs Gorman knew without looking that Don was smiling in sympathy.

'You're both mad,' said Mrs Gorman coldly and began clearing the plates. It wasn't the first time she'd been up against the two of them. There were ways to handle this.

The weeks went by and Mrs Gorman decided that this sudden desire to go to Ireland was nothing more than the last feverish fantasy of a middle-aged man. Nothing prepared her for the 7th August 1981 when he announced that the business was sold and the house was on the market. She remembered sitting opposite him in a matching armchair, listening to him telling her, looking at his face as though she hated him.

He had brought them here and within a year Lizzie had gone and now he was dead. He had disappeared, gone to ground, left her in this bedroom trying to sleep with the house full of his relatives.

As a child she had this dream. She would be running down the street to her house having to get home, desperate because something was chasing her. When she was at the door she'd pound and pound with the knocker until the door opened. But it was another woman, not her mother, who answered and this woman didn't know her and wouldn't let her in.

She had come here. She had not complained. She passed no comment on the TV personalities that no one had ever heard of and politicians with unpronounceable names. She learned to translate their dialect, to accustom herself to the twisting twanging accents of a people who spoke English neither as foreigners nor as the English would themselves. She stayed firm in the face of their effusive, excessive, possibly sarcastic politeness. There was no chance of her being belittled by them. And if they spoke too quickly, rushing along through stories, endless stories that never seemed finished at the end, she endured it as she endured their habit of breaking into maudlin song in public at the flimsiest excuse.

The worst moments were when surrounded by familiar names, Marks and Spencers, MacDonalds, British Home Stores, she would find herself pushing through the crowds on O'Connell Street forgetting she was not in England. At the bridge, when the realisation hit her, she would stand stock still as the crowds banged into her and past her. Over the rail the river didn't look like water, it was too green, too different, another element entirely.

There were times when Don was alive that it took all her self-control not to round on him, not to scream that she was sick of his family trailing through the house day and night, the women crowded into the kitchen when she was trying to cook and the men trying to persuade Don out to the pub. It was all a subterfuge, a sham, with their currency looking like real money but not quite, an unreal city with people who never seemed genuine, who clearly weren't. All of this she lived with, and then one day he went for his customary walk along the canal and didn't come back. It was as simple, as effective as that.

'I'll come home. I'll come back,' Lizzie had cried over the phone when her mother had finally tracked her down at the hospital.

'There's no need,' said Mrs Gorman.

'I can get over by —'

'It'd cost a fortune and they probably don't fly direct to Dublin,' said Mrs Gorman.

'They do.'

'Do they? The funeral's the day after tomorrow. You'd never get back in time, you know that.'

I can't believe it. Just walking, for Christ's sake. Just taking a bloody walk.' Lizzie's voice threatened to go on and on.

'You're a grown woman,' Mrs Gorman reminded her. 'These things happen.'

When Mrs Gorman put down the receiver at the end of the conversation she was surprised to realise how her hand was aching. Either she'd been gripping the receiver very hard or her rheumatism was beginning very early this year. There were more important things to worry about.

There is always a great deal to do after a death and to do quickly. The arrangements for the funeral itself she left in Martin's hands as she wanted no complaints or comments from anyone. There would be "little occasion for financial worry for the foreseeable future" the lawyer said, in his lawyerly way permitting himself a small but not exuberant smile. It surprised her to realise how heavily Don had insured his life.

Then there were the letters to write to inform those who had a right to know and to thank those who had sent their condolences. These she read quickly and threw away. The house got a thorough clear out. Oxfam's done well, she wrote to Lizzie in that jocular style of hers. Systematically his suits, his pipe, his wood-working tools were disposed of. There isn't any sense in dwelling in the past. Besides, she disliked suddenly coming across something of his, a handkerchief, letters addressed to him. It did no good. It wasn't easy, there were always things turning up, like that tub of smokers' tooth powder in the bathroom cabinet. It had rolled out from behind the shampoo one morning and fell, scattering its contents all over the carpet. She could have screamed.

The days did seem empty, without structure as the spring of routine uncoiled. Across the room in the evenings, the chair that Don had sat on seemed to have grown, to assert itself unnecessarily. She went for long walks, painted the kitchen in a new shade of lemon and began to think seriously about looking for a part-time job, an interest.

'I have decided not to go back to England. Six years is too long. There's nothing for me there now. I must make the best of it, that's all. Don's family are very kind and would be here every day if I let them. I've had the kitchen redecorated. As to to coming home that's nonsense. You've a good job out there. You must make a life for yourself. There's no work over here I can tell you. I can't imagine why you want a photograph of a tombstone. You're a strange girl. Besides there isn't one up yet. They have to wait for the earth to settle first. If it's put in too soon it'll go crooked.'

Every Thursday morning Mrs Gorman posted a letter to Lizzie, it was important to keep in contact. She even began going to church again, the walk was pleasant and it was never crowded inside. It had been years and years since she'd been a churchgoer. Once she'd remarked that she'd been brought up a Methodist and Ray, Martin's son, had made some remark about Paisley.

On Tuesday she would drive to the supermarket and do the shopping when the place was quiet. Afterwards she'd stop for a coffee. She found herself eating one, often two buns, sticky with cream and jam. It was true she was eating more. She wasn't hungry. It was as if there was a baby starving to death in her belly and she must feed it at all costs. Some of her skirts stopped fitting her.

She spent hours thinking things over. Before he died she'd been very homesick she realised. It was curious really to remember. It didn't matter now if she never moved again and she was sure she'd never go back home. The fact she hated this country ceased to trouble her.

There was nothing to be done about that. On Friday mornings she went regularly to the hairdressers. 'Keeping up appearances', she'd say to herself with a grim smile. There could be no denying, she'd regained any grip she'd lost over her life. The dust had settled.

Then one day she was standing in the kitchen rinsing out an omelette pan with very hot water and the very next moment she was lying on the floor, her cheek resting on the stone-colour cushioned flooring. She lay there dazed, dumped out of her own element, on eye level with the doormat. Slowly she got to her feet, gripping the rim of the stainless-steel sink until the rings on her fingers cut into her. The side of her face, her cheekbone ached. Her heart was pumping like a new battery in an old body. She could do nothing until its rhythm slowed, just breathe quickly, heavily. When she had recovered she made herself a cup of coffee, sat down, drank it.

She half forgot the incident until she saw her face in the bathroom mirror that night. The bruise was already visible. She touched it, stared at it, surprised by its appearance on that most intimate self, the face. Anyone would think she'd been in a boxing match, she had to laugh. Laughing, she saw how white and drained her gums looked. She resolved, next morning, to make an appointment with the dentist. Retracted gums can mean lost teeth. Lizzie had been made to go to the dentist every three months without fail. In the waiting-room Mrs Gorman had read the notices of what to watch for and one of them was gum disease. She switched off the bathroom light.

Next day she hadn't planned to go out anyway and by Wednesday the swelling had disappeared. After a careful application of foundation there was absolutely nothing to be seen. Mrs Gorman did not normally wear very much in the way of make-up. War paint her mother had called it, but she'd been very old-fashioned.

Cissy called round in the afternoon. Mrs Gorman had got her into the habit of phoning first. She was a great talker, she chattered about family, about friends, about strangers. Mrs Gorman sat back in the armchair listening.

'I don't know what you mean, Mrs Gorman, the manager said with a real face on him,' Cissy went on.

Mrs Gorman was jolted by the sound of her name. ' Pardon? '

'At the cleaners, about Martin's suit,' explained Cissy. "I don't know what you mean Mrs Gorman,' he said. 'I think we've done an excellent job given the age of the garment," Cissy snorted. 'Garment! He was twenty two if he was a day.'

'Who was?'

'The manager,' said Cissy.

There was a moment's silence. Mrs Gorman was wondering why it had never occurred to her that Cissy was called Mrs Gorman as well. It just never had. She got up and said at random, 'Shall I make a cup of tea?'

'Don't go to any bother now," said Cissy meekly or sarcastically, Mrs Gorman was too tired to distinguish.

At least Cissy left early that afternoon. She fumbled at the buckle of her mauve mac in the hallway, looking awkward. The raincoat did not suit her.

'Goodbye Cissy,' said Mrs Gorman, opening the front door for her.

Cissy seized her hand. 'You take care now Rose. Why don't you call over and have your Sunday dinner with us? It'd be a change. You're always more than welcome. You know that. I hope you know that."

'That's very kind of you.'

'We'll expect you then?' asked Cissy, not letting go of her hand.

'We'll see,' said Mrs Gorman as she used to say to Lizzie when she meant no.

It was on Sunday that it happened again. She was in the hallway just about to put on her coat and go to church when she found herself blinking slowly up at the ceiling. Her ankle had twisted badly. She didn't know what had happened. One moment she was perfectly alright and the next levelled to the floor. There was nothing wrong with her, she was sure of that. It was as though someone had sneaked up behind her and, with a weapon or bare-handed, clubbed her down. Mrs Gorman didn't want to be frightened. She got into the car and drove to church defiantly, her shoulders squared, her back rigid.

It happened again during the week, twice the next week. Once she came-to leaning against a wall with people crowded around her and an ambulance called for. It was enough to make her afraid to go out. She'd managed to get away that time but in the future who could tell. There was something about hospitals she hated. Of course her appearance suffered. There were bruises old and new on her body, her face. One Friday she'd had to cancel her appointment with the hairdressers she looked so bad. It was a shame that she had to lie to the doctor when she at last decided to have a check-up. She told him she'd slipped on a stair-rod and fell. There was nothing wrong with her heart, her blood pressure, anything, and that was a relief.

'You'd need to lose a little of that weight,' he said. ' Aside from that you're as sound as a bell. ' He flicked his forefinger against the coffee mug on the desk. It pinged.

Round the house she walked more stiffly, more erect, refusing to give way. In the streets people parted before her. If it had been summer she might have worn sun-glasses. Her face had a naked, battered look and she sometimes could not face taking it into the outside world. She would sit in the lounge and read the newspaper that was delivered every day. Of course she was tempted to write something to Lizzie, even to phone her, but what could she say that would make sense? There was nothing she could say that would make sense.

The day she was due to go to the dentist, she went face down on the bedroom floor. Her upper lip was crushed and swollen, even after the ice had cooled down the worst of it, it looked and felt sore. She looked at herself in the mirror. She waited for herself to speak.

'Why are you doing this Don?' she asked. ' Why? ' And as though sounding an unfamiliar note she said his name again, 'Don.' From her body bloomed the most bitter grief. The house that had been empty was full. It was full to overflowing. For the first time since his death Mrs Gorman lay down and wept.

Last Days

'Good luck,' they called, leaning over the side of the ship.

She could think of nothing to say.

'Good luck,' they said again, their faces kind and ironical.

The waves were worrying, fidgeting at her small wooden boat. Of all of them only the face of the man who had been her lover was serious, even glum. That would be noticed and later on he would be reasoned with. Never again would they reason with her, she thought, getting a half-ashamed sense of pleasure from that idea. At least not for a long time. She fixed the oars in position and, with her back to the ship, began the steady pull to the shore.

They had not warned her that it would be as warm as this. Within minutes the shirt was sweated to her back. The water got thicker, the oars heavier, until the boat was scarcely moving at all. She looked over her shoulder with disfavour at the neat rubber-packed boxes bobbing blackly in her wake. They were so many anchors weighing her down, dragging at her, or perhaps they were a lifeline, a last contact with the civilised world. To cut that cord, she thought, to float free in this muddy indistinct world between mist and water, sea and shore, without rhyme or reason . . . She bent back into the oars. She must arrive before the tide turned or be driven back out to sea. That was enough to concentrate on, this was no time to run through her future plans, the sway and push of the boat was repetitious, inhibiting thought.

Landfall was a small jetty, half-submerged by water. There was nobody there, nobody to greet her. That was to be expected of course, even if they were still capable of maintaining a watch it would not be on this side of the island. They would look for rescue or for relief from the mainland, if they still entertained such hopes. It was hard to find a place to land, the steps, the metal rungs, the jetty itself were all covered in a sodden fur of green weed. It clung vivid and voracious everywhere the water reached. Once on shore it took time to decide which of the broken-down buildings was usable as a storeroom. Then came the task of hauling the boxes out of the water and half lifting, half dragging the boxes there. All this required patience, but long ago she had accepted the value of hard monotonous work done for a reason. Yet it did no harm to recite those reasons aloud. Next it was time to sit on an old concrete block letting her muscles relax, her breathing ease. There was nothing to be seen except the white wall of mist with a grey scrabble of water underneath.

If there had been a map, she thought as she prepared to walk inland rucksack on back, if there had been a map, no matter how inaccurate, how confused, even incomprehensible . . . But there were no maps, or if there were they had not been given to her. She must just walk until she found a settlement, and which direction? North, due North. She had not asked her instructor why North, because she could not bear the expression on his face, the way he shrugged when he said, why not? She knew better than to provoke responses that she could not deal with. That was a lesson learned in kindergarten.

The settlement was not hard to find. The smoke from the fire was visible for miles. Warily she went forward, taking time, her senses on high alert. None of this was necessary, she realised, as she watched from the shadow of an old wrecked wall the dispirited, dishevelled group gathered there. Even the fire was a loose sprawling mess, taking up too much room, giving off too much smoke. It wasn't there for warmth, it was hours till noon and already the air was close. They were not using it to cook food, for the light it gave, for the comfort, or even to signal their distress. It was there purely to waste wood, or so it seemed.

So with her hands loose and empty and with her face expressionless she walked out into open view. For a few seconds she did nothing, did not even glance in their direction.

'Hello,' she said quietly. 'I am a friend.'

There was the faintest sound, as if someone turned, as if someone had reacted. She almost felt a rush of excitement but her training held and the adrenalin didn't have time to take effect. Here and now could well be the turning point in her life, in all their lives, there was no excuse for indulging in excitement or anticipation.

Moving very slowly, in order to cause them no alarm and in order to maintain a vigilant eye on her own responses, she walked towards the fire. Now was the time to perform a simple, easily understandable action. She took the rucksack from her back and unbuckled it. From its wide open throat she took a bag of dried food and a metal container. Next she mixed the dried food with water from her canteen. The small gas cooker she carried was quick and efficient. Within minutes the smell of hot food was in the air. At no point did she even glance at them, not even at the child she could hear whimpering with hunger. In leisurely fashion she ate her bowl of food and sat back on her heels.

'Hot food,' she remarked to no one in particular, 'hot food is very good.'

There was no response. To her right an old woman lay, her hair flaked with ashes from the fire; it was impossible to know if she was awake or asleep. It was difficult but she managed not to feel the impulse towards revulsion and pity. It was better to pour another bowl of food and to begin eating that in a bored way. Halfway through she paused, yawned, and very deliberately slopped the contents of the bowl in the dust between her feet. She even scooped the remains out with her fingers and flicked little globules of food at the people around her. She thought she detected a slight tensing in the atmosphere.

A young man leaned forward and spat into the fire. The spit sizzled. It was not, she knew, a gesture of aggression towards her, it was not anger at someone wasting food in the presence of people who were clearly starved with hunger. It was only that the sight and smell of food had stimulated his body to produce saliva to the point of excess, and this he had discarded probably without thinking. Still it was a response and one that she must capitalise on immediately.

'Would you like to eat?' she asked the young man.

For a while he sat, his face contorted and then he said, 'Yes.'

It was so much more than she expected, that they would actually speak, actually use words to her, that only years of discipline kept her from crying out, from clapping her hands or laughing.

Now that one of them had indicated that he wanted food, she could feed them all. For some it must have been many days since their last meal but they ate lazily, with disinterest. She watched them, seeing that there were no children under the age of five and only eight women of child-bearing age, that the surviving old people were in various extremes of malnutrition and despair, and that of the five men none was younger than twenty-five. They were clearly on the edge of viability. There was much to be done. Across her shoulders a hot bar of sunlight burned.

After her tent was erected and various enticing objects left around to stimulate and test their curiosity, it was time to begin her exercises. Nothing could be more important than these daily, exhaustive, self-examinations.

First she must ensure that her physical health was on course, that her suppleness, her co-ordination had not suffered change.

'Your body can at any time create the conditions for your personality's collapse,' she said softly to herself, running the familiar words over her tongue, absorbing them. Without constant vigilance could come those upsurges of emotion, anger, hatred, love that have overwhelmed so many good hardworking people. Of course they had received treatment, but the impairment was permanent. Thinking of that she picked up her various textbooks, read, answered set questions, checked her results, wrote her diary and generally maintained mental hygiene.

They had touched nothing. Not the bright coloured scarves, the sugar, the bottle of alcohol, the shiny knife, nothing. It didn't appear that they had moved at all in the time she'd been busy. It was to be expected. The next move would be to go over to the young man who had spoken before. She squatted in the dust in front of him as he sat trying to balance stones on top of one another.

'Hello,' she said. 'I am a friend.'

There was no interest, no reaction.

'I am your friend. I have come from a long way away. I have come to help you.'

He scratched the inside of his ear as though it irritated him. She took a piece of sugar from her pocket and forced it between his teeth. His eyes widened with surprise. He began to suck noisily.

'I am your friend,' she repeated, trying to establish an association between her presence and the sweetness of sugar in his mind. With a hand under his chin she forced him to look at her. When she smiled, he smiled. When she stood up, he copied her, even brushing the back of his rags free of dust in imitation of her.

'There are people here who need medicine.' Not that he would understand these words but she wanted to accustom him to the sound of her voice, to remind him of language. After all he had remembered one word and that could be built on. 'I have medicine. You and I will go and get the medicine.'

As long as she held his hand it was easy to persuade him to trot obediently at her side. He walked with his head bowed, with dirty fair hair flopping over his neck. It was so frail a neck, it could be snapped like the stalk of a reed, leaving the head to loll grotesquely unconnected to the spine. She swallowed and made them both run faster.

The supplies they collected kept the camp going for many days. With good food, medicine, the edge of their listlessness and apathy blunted. After a while it became possible to persuade some of them to help her prepare and serve the food. Even the children's appearance improved. They had the energy now to run hooting round the camp like wild animals. It was enough to break your heart. Now that they were healthy the signs of the degenerative disease were even easier to see.

They obeyed her every instruction as well as they could. It was impossible to imagine a more tractable group of people than these. She did not reproach them for their ineptitude, they did what they could, she reasoned. And if the attempt to plant crops failed because none of them, not even the young man, could remember to irrigate, to hoe . . . very well, they could turn to a more ancient tradition. That was where she would draw the starting line. They would be hunters.

'We have very little time,' she would say to him. 'If only you could realise how very little time we have.' He would look at her and she would sigh.

Of course she knew how necessary it was for the tribe to resume sexual activity. Dying out was no answer to the disease, but it was difficult to persuade him to make love either publicly or privately. At night he slept, during the day he wanted the drudgery of work or to be left alone. Still, with patience, it was done. Afterwards his eyes looked dark and bewildered. She left the tent and began immediately, with the assistance of a detailed question-naire, to assess her mental state. They had explained to her the rewards and penalties of her position. She must check that she was on target.

Then she could lie back in the hot dry grass and feel the ants swarm into her hair. She didn't mind, she was making the pattern of star constellations appear and disappear at will. It was the first lesson she had learned, that only with effort, continuous effort, does meaning assert itself. Orion's belt burned bluely, and that was a good omen for a hunting people. Tomorrow she would take the most able-bodied of them with her and teach them how to stalk and how to kill. But now thinking of him she was wondering if they had been right about her ability to endure. There was an urge in her to cry out, to weep.

'Alone,' she whispered. 'All alone.' She made her face twist into a sarcastic smile.

At home, in the city, only those most adept, whose emotions were well dulled by training, years of training, were ever left alone. The young were always kept in company, there hatred, excessive affection, anger could all be monitored by instructors, or group-monitored as they themselves grew older. For a person alone there was fear, there was loneliness, there was despair and all these must be suppressed not faced. The temptation was always to deal with these terrible emotions, nothing was more impossible, more foolhardy. The best of them had been lost that way.

There was no knowing now how or where the degenerative disease had begun. There had been so many new sicknesses, some that attacked the immune system, some that corrupted the function of the central nervous system. There came the rapid cancer, the A form meningitis that left its survivors with all the symptoms of late-stage schizophrenia. It was all the fault of the scientists, the governments, it was nature acting in revulsion, or just an accident, a series of coincidences. Millions might die but always, always, came the cure and with the cures new possibilities, a remedy for mortality itself. It was a dream to obsess and mesmerise while quietly, unnoticed, the real enemy had slipped behind the undefended lines.

When it was recognised, when they had given it a name it had already inserted itself inside the genetic structure of most of the planet's population. There, in the individual cell, it began its work of decay. All that was needed, past its period of seemingly necessary dormancy, was the physiological stimulus associated with strong emotion. It didn't matter what the feeling was, fear could be the trigger or grief. The degenerative effect from each attack was cumulative and permanent. Children were born with the precise characteristics of their mothers' devolution. Amongst the survivors a marked reluctance to reproduce was noted. Even in the City itself, that last stronghold of old learning, children were rare and getting rarer.

What could be done? Consolidate where possible. Conserve where possible. Watch with as little emotion as possible the grotesque deaths and even more bizarre lives of those who endured the disease. Sit and wait as the Romans waited, as the Aztecs waited, for the barbarians to come, but this time they would not come from outside the walls, from another country. Every moment must be accounted for, occupied. All the roads to excess must be blocked. Order and discipline and a life-enhancing dullness would be the only way the City could survive. But still there were fewer children born and even fewer women who survived childbirth intact. Something must be done.

'Do you ever wonder about me?' she asked. 'Wonder who I am, what I'm doing here?'

They were sitting on the jetty and he was weaving reeds to make a strong pliable basket in the way that she'd taught him. The smell of mud was overpowering.

'No,' he said truthfully.

'Do you never ask why I came to help you, what advantage I am looking for?'

He looked embarrassed and then he looked away. She should know better than to torment him with the larger issues, the ones he was incapable of understanding. There was a restlessness in her that would have worried her instructors.

'If I hadn't come you would have died. All of you would have died. Of malnutrition, of despair, of the disease. You needn't die of the disease, it needn't destroy you. We have a method. We have a way.' She smiled boastfully and put her hand on his arm.

'You give us presents,' he said.

'Yes, I give you presents,' she agreed, and stroked his hair. She caught herself wondering again what he had been like before the disease and how it was he had suffered so little impairment. It must be because he had accepted the situation. Even now he never complained at the drudgery and austerity of the life she imposed on them. For days she had led them out, inland, to stalk the half-wild cattle. She had watched closely for signs of enthusiasm or resentment. There were none. Their indifference and her unrelenting control were both techniques for survival, she would remind herself. He had fallen asleep curled up at her feet. She didn't mind. She watched the sea shifting restlessly in its bed like someone too tired to sleep.

After a while she bent down and touched his shoulder.

'We have things in the store house we must take back to the camp. I have a new present for you,' she said to him. 'Something for hunting.'

Obediently he got up and followed her, his half-finished basket abandoned. They had both forgotten it.

Between them they managed to get the long wooden boxes to the camp, he panting heavily with exertion and she taking the opportunity to recite the first book of the Iliad, as much as she could remember. The need to memorise, to remember was a paramount duty. So much had been lost, was being lost. In the library she had even seen the best instructors turn over the pages of a book with incomprehension on their faces. This was a duty she must not neglect, not even here. It was almost like having a conversation with another person.

They lowered the box in front of the firecircle she had

marked for them with white stones. No detail could be neglected in the pursuit of order. She waited for the whole group to gather, she looked at them with pride. So much had been achieved, there was even one woman pregnant. The bodies of the children were stronger even if their eyes were only fitfully human.

'I am your friend.' She began the familiar ritual and most of them remembered to nod in agreement. Then she used one of her many tools to carefully lever up the nailed-down lid of the box. It broke open.

'Metal,' said one of the old people.

'Guns,' she corrected. 'Guns to hunt with.'

First she showed them how to load, aim and fire and then to reload the rifle. She showed them again. Then again. She gave sugar to the ones who remembered best. It took days before she would allow any of them to come hunting with her. The first day the hunters returned, she made sure herself that there was an animal to carry home. They needed that encouragement, she decided. They would improve with practice. Everybody liked the meat. The children, in particular, liked to lick the blood from each other's downy faces. That night in exultant mood she said to them:

'We will hunt. There is always food for hunters. We have these guns, these bullets. My friends will give us more, they will send us more. And we will build huts, houses. We will have a good life.'

Before she knew it she was on her feet and dancing. These were her people and she had rescued them and now she would teach them a new life.

'Dance,' she commanded the young man.

His body moved awkwardly, unnaturally against her. He was patient; there were times when it seemed he needed a violent action to make him react. Unfortunately nobody with her education ever used violence. It was true in the time that followed she thought less, she cared less about the reasons they had given for sending her here. There was the memory of the way they had leaned over the side of the ship and blessed her. And although their precise instructions escaped her there was no doubt that she had been sent to help and for that help she would be rewarded. It was harder now for her to spend the hours required at reading, at writing. In her sleep she heard the creak of leather, felt the dried stalks of grass under her feet and the sudden instinctive flash of rifle fire as another hunt came to culmination. When, that winter, the woman gave birth, she didn't inspect the child for signs or symptoms. Neither did she ask herself to explain that reluctance.

One morning she was sitting face to face with the sea. The wind was coming up with the faintest tang of rain in it. Idly she flung stone after stone into the reeds. Her mind was calm and blank. This afternoon she would take them hunting, she decided, rubbing her shoulder from the memory of the rifle's recoil. It was strange that the relationship between the rifle and herself could trigger the death of any animal. Then she heard him coming up behind her.

'Yes?' she said and motioned him to be seated.

His face was flat and unreadable in the early morning light. She was reminded, uneasily, of another face leaning from the side of a ship, a man who had also been her lover. There was no connection between that man and this man except herself. Left alone they were worlds apart, she was the only point at which they met. They would never meet. Abruptly birds levitated out of the water, into the air, their cries curiously muffled.

'I wish,' she said dreamily. 'I wish that I could fly like that.'

He waited until she had finished speaking, then said, 'I have been thinking.'

It was a phrase she often used, she smiled at him affectionately. 'That's good.'

'Look,' he said, and he laid his gun down on the ground between them.

'It is a gun,' she said, thinking perhaps that for a moment he had forgotten.

Quickly he nodded his head. 'It is a gun. For

hunting.

Picking up the gun he went through the motions of aiming, shooting and reloading. It was a pity his movements were so clumsy, so graceless. Even the faintest hint of the disease seemed to wither up finesse. Sometimes she even noticed in herself a little clumsiness.

'You see,' he said triumphantly as the rifle dropped to the ground and became splattered with mud.

'Pick it up,' she said sternly.

'All that for such a simple thing.' He was nearly shouting, she wasn't sure if he had ever done that before. 'And the pellets.'

'Bullets,' she corrected automatically.

He was too enthralled to pay much attention to her. 'I have a surprise.'

He walked only a few yards away, bent down, picked up some long object and walked back with it in his hand.

'I took a gun and I put it in the fire for a while. A long while. The fire was very hot. I pulled it out and it was just soft enough to bend and I did bend it and here it is.'

He took the shapeless club of metal and banged it down again and again, making the noise of a rifle firing. That way he killed three imaginary animals before stopping to smile at her.

'No spare parts,' he said, using another expression of hers.

'Have you done this to all the guns,' she asked without emotion in her voice.

'Not all the guns.'

Slowly she ran her hand down the dark wood stock of her rifle. 'Then the best thing,' she said, clearly enunciating her words, 'is to go back to the compound to do the same thing to all the other guns you can find. Here.'

Grinning with delight, he took the burnt gun from her outstretched hands and with his new club at a jaunty angle over his shoulder began to walk back to the camp. She sat without moving or thinking. Then her hands snapped open her own rifle and very precisely extracted each bullet from its inside. The rifle lay across her knees dead and broken. She took the bullets from her belt, weighed them in her hand, licked them to get their true taste. Then she flung them as she had flung the stones earlier. They crashed into the reeds.

They would never come back for her now. She would never signal for them. Under the shock of her failure she knew how ridiculous had been her dream to create a tribe of happy hunters. That had not been her task, she had created her own task and injected these people with that creativeness. She had seen the look in his eyes. First he had invented the club. In a little while they would discover stone, the flint axe. Then one day these would invent fire, they would not cease now from the urgent need to discover and create. She had unleashed that and the time would come when they would take that giant leap from the grassland to the trees. Already the signs were there, even without the benefit of her exacerbation. Perhaps she was only hastening the inevitable.

It would be a swift disintegration, a picture returned to her of the last child born. Once the use of language had lapsed those changes would accelerate. The individual consciousness that each one possessed would concentrate, then blank out.

'Innocent. Innocent,' she said, grinding the words with her teeth.

The central nervous system would simplify and simplify as the limbs retracted and foreshortened. Fur would flourish as never before. They would seek shelter in the roots of trees, between rocks. At all events they would remain a herd. It was possible, in generations to come, they would cease to be vertebrates at all. Their skeletons would be squeezed out of them, surrounding them in a thin crust of shell.

That would be punishment enough. To be marooned here, the only human being in an island of crawling pink crablike creatures. Except that she was no longer separate, her controls had long ago fallen into disuse. When the time came she would be with them here on this foreshore, in whatever form. She would go back with them to their first element, the sea. It would be a tender homecoming.